Linda J Pifer

DANIEL SMITH

New Zealand Passage

This is a work of fiction. Names, characters, places and incidents are the product of the author's imagination and are used fictitiously. Any resemblance to actual persons, living or dead, events, or locales is entirely coincidental.

Cover photos – Dreamstime.com

Cover design by Linda J Pifer

Published by Readingseat Books – An LLC Company

ISBN: 978-0-9890142-3-6

Preface

The fiction genealogy story of the Smith family, introduced in 'Windows' continues as Daniel Smith, their 5th removed grandfather leaves Scotland's great poverty of 1847 to emigrate to New Zealand.

Daniel arrives by tall ship determined to succeed as he steps ashore, but he encounters more hardships than Aberdeen's emigration posters described. Strengths and weaknesses are tested as he works to establish a new life and tap into the country's rich farmland.

Danger, personal loss, true friendship, love and hope all play a part in Daniel's surprising story, a rich and life-renewing tale.

Look For Other Books
From Linda J Pifer

Ohio Girl

A memoir of childhood and family in Ohio;
Illus. 92 vintage pictures, 122 pages

Windows

Book One in the Windows Trilogy
Follow an American widow to the U.K.
where she begins her genealogic research
for the Smith family at their country manor
and becomes forever-entwined
in their history.

Visit the author's website at:
http://www.lindajpiferauthor.com

To The One over all of us

And to those who surround me
and make life so fine;
My Family;
John Roger
Susan and Damon,
Sarah and John
Linda and Bobby and Ariana
Mom Marin
Aunt Olive
And all the Guerin clan.

Chapter 1   Arrival - April 18, 1848

The calm blue harbor stretches for miles around me as I turn full circle to gaze from the ship's rail. We lay at final mooring on New Zealand's south island as early morning fog lifts and hangs just behind the western mountains. To the east, rolling hills and distant peaks gleam in the morning sun and I shield my eyes against its brightness.

We've lived at sea more than three months since sailing from Greenock and it's strange to see the hint of fall color on the hills of the Peninsula. We left Scotland last November and I struggle to adjust to the new timetable, now the seasons are turned opposite.

Though anxious to be off the ship, I suspect it'll be another hour or more before our hundred-odd passengers are safely ashore. Meanwhile, the people below on the wharf offer me entertainment as vendors crowd in to press their wares.

"PotatŌ" one calls out and I watch him take a steaming hot yam wrapped in a leaf from an earthenware crock then hold it aloft.

"Hapenny" he calls again and more than one passenger buys while still onboard; a coin tossed to the vendor results in a potato thrown high over the rail to be grabbed out of the air.

All manner of characters stand about, most dressed in their best with small baggage, waiting to board for the next port of Melbourne. Children dodge in and out during a rowdy game of tag and evoke my smile. Their activity creates frequent outbursts of indignation like that of the matron just now, who scolds loudly after being rudely jabbed by an errant elbow; her ample figure taking up more than her share of space on the dock.

Burlap-wrapped bundles of sheep skins, supplies for the ship and wooden crates stacked high alongside us for the next port provide makeshift seating for the dock crew who wait for the bosom's signal to load.

At the head of the wharf, ragtag bunches of men with dog and mule carts vie for the best spots and wait to transport passenger trunks. Several locals watch our masted ship from onshore at the water's edge and seem amused by the circus-like scene as they laugh and point.

I trace the sea gulls' flight overhead as they dive at vendors' baskets and fight over dropped morsels. They cheer their own success in a cacophony of outcries while the ever present smell of fish mixed with the odor of the harbor assaults my nostrils. Altogether, it's a sensory overload after our months at sea.

"Daniel Smith to the plank." The bosom orders me out over the general clamor from his place atop a chair.

Roused abruptly, I answer with a yell loud enough to be heard; "Here!" and hastily take my wife's arm to propel her across the wooden deck.

"Here, Sir." I say again as we stand in front of the ship's first officer. The Lieutenant turns to Rose and asks "Rose Smith?"

She trembles a little at my arm but replies "Yes." He checks both our names off the manifest then smiles and touches the brim of his hat.

"Good luck to you both, a safe passage." Having said, he turns to read off the next name to his bosun.

We pass from the sea to land with little fanfare; it's a let-down of sorts I think. I'm so exhilarated to finally reach the shore that surely, fireworks would be appropriate. The giddiness in the pit of my stomach makes me smile but the gravity of our decision to leave all we've known settles suddenly upon me like a blanket softening the noise around me.

I wonder if we'll ever see our parents again and the hardships of our voyage run briefly through my mind like a kaleidoscope; crowded space with strangers, seasickness, tempers flaring with the climate change and food rations during our last days at sea.

Abruptly I return to the present and fight down my doubts. There will be hard months ahead but failure is not a word I'll use again in my life, though this mantra of sorts will probably be repeated many times.

Rose's lovely blue eyes look up to question my hesitation and I answer with a confident smile, "Ready?"

She returns my smile in kind; "Aye Daniel" she says and with a last look around the deck, we descend the gangplank together.

Our first step onto the solidness of the wharf throws us both slightly off-balance and she reaches for me to steady herself.

"Oh Daniel, I am so glad to be off that ship."

"Aye, so am I."

We stand looking around as we find ourselves smack in the middle of the crowd we watched from the rail.

"Come with me." I pull her past and through the people to settle her on a shipping crate at the edge of the wharf.

"You stay here and get rid of your sea legs while I attend to our trunks."

I turn back to the noisy crowd but come up short, to stare straight into the eyes of the strangest man I've ever seen. He's a dark-skinned native, his tattooed face surrounded by long black hair and entwined with feathers and green stone ornaments. His clothing is limited to a feather-trimmed leather vest and a pair of loosely draped trousers in coarse woven linen. He stands solidly without yielding, as if he is the only one here and his right hand grips a tall walking stick festooned with like decorations.

"Excuse me sir, may I pass?" He answers only with a deep-throated "Hmmf." Deciding it's a 'yes', I nod then proceed around him to our trunks.

I watch Daniel make his way back through the crowd and notice the native he's just passed is now staring at me. I look away and feign interest in other people, but he continues to stare. I begin to tremble a little until I think; this is ridiculous, take control of the situation and speak to him, though I doubt he'll understand me.

He stops in front of me; "Hello, I'm Rose."

"Hmmf" He grunts in reply but all the while he seems to be looking at my hat and even points to it. I point to my little woven straw decorated with painted flowers and wide blue ribbon; "This?" I ask.

"Hmmf"

Not wishing to offend him, I remove the pin and hold the hat out to him. He takes it, turns it this way and that then puts it on his head.

"Oh." I say in disappointment, discretely hiding the word behind my hand and realise now my hat won't be back on my head. But on the positive side, he does seem quite pleased with it.

He reacts to my muffled comment and reaches into the bag over his shoulder to pull out a talisman of the same green stone as his hair ornaments. He quickly hands it to me and turns away into the crowd before I can say more. I look down at object in my hand and there are carvings. When I hold it up to the sun, veins of a lighter green color shoot through its translucent dark green. How beautiful I think and hang it around my neck by its braided leather strap.

Daniel soon returns with our trunks piled high on the smallest wagon I've ever seen and pulled by, of all things, two large white goats. Their owner is a blonde young laddie of about twelve who holds the bridle of one animal to guide both and urges them on with a light tap from a switch.

"Rose, this is James Ferguson our porter." Daniel looks at me more closely, "Where's your hat? The sun's getting hot."

"Well, I think I've made my first trade here in New Zealand."

His expression is one of incomprehension and he continues, "Let's find the Land Office before we decide where to stay tonight. James, can you take us there?"

"Yes sir, follow me." James answers.

I realise Daniel's preoccupied with our arrival and I drop the subject until a better time and follow Daniel and our lively young porter up the dirt road ahead of us into the settlement.

Other passengers we recognize are walking in the same direction and dust from the road begins to billow. At one point I help push our wagon up the increasing incline ahead of us.

There were few signs of civilization around the shores of the harbor as we entered, but here there are several cabins and roughly built wooden buildings with a few more scattered over the hills above.

A gentle breeze blows up and over us to sway the tall trees above the settlement. It's a paradise I think as I continue to walk wearily up the main road and struggle to keep up with my husband and the boy.

With a glance back at Rose, I tell James to continue on and stop to take her arm. The townspeople are watching from their boardwalks and porches as if we're on parade.

"Are you alright?" I ask her; beads of perspiration lie on her forehead.

"They don't get this many people arriving every day do they Daniel?" She remarks and holds to my arm.

"Probably not."

"And as to your question, yes I'm fine; just a little overheated and dusty."

"We'll find a place to stop soon and get some water." I tell her and notice many settlers are dressed in work clothes as they pause from loading their wagons to stare at us. The local smithy seems quite busy but his customers turn to watch.

An older man of about fifty mingles up ahead of us and slowly works his way back through the people in our 'parade'. He's tall and craggy, dressed in work trousers, a plaid shirt and vest. His beard and gray hair wave about as he goes from person to person to greet them and when he approaches us, his hand is extended, his words spoken loudly.

"Welcome, I'm Mayor MacDougal, Ronan for my friends, which I consider you two to be." He shakes my hand firmly and nods to Rose which sets his hair to waving even more.

"Where do you hail from?"

"Aberdeen, out of Grenock."

"Splendid. Ah, I miss the old moors of my childhood, but I traded em' long ago for this Eden and I've never regretted it. What's your trade?"

"Quarryman, but lately, raising sheep which we plan to do here. We've rented a farm about five miles away."

"Good for you man, farming is a little different here; you'll find things grow faster, sometimes too fast when it comes to weeds but none-the-less, your labors will pay off. Grand to meet you both, call on me anytime down at the Dockside pub, I'd be pleased to see you." He turns and moves on to the next couple behind us.

Some enthusiasm, I think as we continue to hear his repeated greetings down the long line.

We reach the Land Office at last in its unpainted wooden building and stop to join the line of people already waiting.

"I'll stay with you." James says and parks his wagon near a water bucket where his goats can drink. We take some water to freshen up and wipe the sweat and dust from our faces. Some women from the local church

13

come down the line with biscuits, honey and a water crock and we feel slightly renewed after partaking.

In three hours' time, we're invited into the office at a few minutes to five.

"Mr. MacMillan, I'm Daniel Smith and this is my wife Rose. We corresponded last year."

"Why yes, very nice to meet you. Please have a seat."

His brown suit and white shirt are a little rumpled and he straightens his glasses as he shakes my hand.

"These are our emigration papers," I say as I take them from my jacket pocket, "and the letter you sent about the farm."

"Thank-you. These certainly seem to be in order Daniel, welcome to New Zealand and you too, mam."

"Do you have a map of the property?" I ask.

"Oh yes." He quickly opens a drawer to retrieve one and spreads it open on his desk.

"Now here's our location and here's the farm. It's about five and a half miles from the outskirts of town, just off the main trail to the northeast. The road out is easy to travel this time of year, lucky for you arriving in the fall. Mud will be a problem during our rainy season but you'll learn which routes are best as you go."

"What repairs are needed in general?" I hold my breath as I wait for his answer.

"The house needs some repair of course; you know anything about thatching? The last time I visited, the roof needed considerable work," then he quickly adds, "but the house itself is solid stone."

"I've repaired thatch in my early days; what materials do you use here?"

"We use a long reed grass the Maori call toi-toi; it's easily harvestable and grows in the swampy areas down by the shore.

"Now you'll also find some furniture left behind which should be dried out now as our rainy season has passed. You'll probably need to build a new bed frame since the one I saw is broken, but other than basic supplies and livestock of your choosing, you should be in good stead—some rich grazing pasture right here." He taps an area on the corner of the property then rises from his chair to glance out the window at the line of people waiting.

I pay him the first month's rent and accept the receipt but, though he gives the distinct impression he's finished with us, I persist with a few more questions.

"What about provisions?"

"Of course you'll need basics, tools, nails, wire if you're going to repair fences. Stop by the blacksmith's and talk to Thomas—tell him I said to ask about a wagon and horse. He might know a farmer who can sell you a freshened cow, maybe even some chickens."

"We'll need a place to stay tonight, is there a boarding house?"

"Yes, we have two in town but I fear they're already full at this point considering so many have come at once. If you have blankets, I suggest you choose an out of the way place to erect a tent and bed down for the night. In the morning you can get your supplies, maybe arrange for their delivery."

"Is there a place to eat?" Rose asks.

"Yes mam, turn left out of our door and continue up the hill, you'll see a soup shop run by Muriel Taft. Better hurry, I believe she closes up about seven."

When Rose and I get up to leave he seems pleased and smiles quickly then shows us to the door.

"You'll find folks in town are used to new people more often than those who live outside our settlement. A word of caution, don't wander outside of town without your papers until you're better known hereabouts, understand?"

"Yes, I'll remember." I acknowledge his advice.

He immediately calls in the next couple in line and we are pushed aside as they rush past and close the door.

"Busy man" I comment as we walk up the street with James and the wagon following.

"I think he did the best he could for today Daniel, he's only one man." Rose agrees, "James, do you know where this soup shop is?"

"Oh yeah, it's around the corner here, but I wouldn't eat there."

"Why not?" Rose asks.

"Mum says she's never sure what meat Mrs. Taft puts in the soup" he says with a grimace.

"Oh Daniel, what are we going to do?"

I think for a moment then ask James to take us to the town's Church. He leads us down a side street to a small wood frame building with a steeple where some of the other folks from the ship have already arrived.

"Wait here Rose." The Church's doors are open and I walk up the steps to speak with a man standing outside then quickly return.

"We're here just in time; they have room for one more couple to stay the night. James, I'll give you your pay now and you can go on home. Can you return in the morning to show us around town to the blacksmith and a provisioner?"

"Sure can" he answers happily and accepts the coins I put in his hand.

17

"Good, there'll be extra pay for you if you're here by eight with breakfast, maybe something simple; hardboiled eggs or the like?"

"I'll talk to my Mum, we'll figure something out." James answers.

We unhook the goats and push the wagon to the side of the Church, securing it to the stair rail with rope. I watch James lead his goats home down the small street and silently decide to spend the night on the porch later to watch our trunks; no use taking chances I think, this is all we own in the world.

The ladies of the congregation provided an earlier supper but plenty of left-overs still remain when we join the others inside.

We're pleased to see the modest interior is spotless and a welcome sign has been hung over the door. The floor is scrubbed clean and we admire the wooden pews and the simple altar. The preacher works his way over to us as he greets each new family and leads us in a prayer of thanksgiving for our safe journey. He blesses the food for, as he calls us, 'the town's new friends."

After we eat, Rose settles down on one of the pews with her blanket and pillow. I watch over her and make sure she's sound asleep before slipping away to the front porch. Wrapping up in a blanket, I lean against

18

the wall to enjoy the peace of the evening but thoughts of our voyage crowd in.

Rose's struggle with seasickness in those first weeks was frightening and my worst fear was she would starve. I fed her chicken broth to keep her strength up and licorice candy, when I could get it, to help settle her stomach. Both seemed to help as my mum said they would but, at times all she could keep down was dry bread and water.

One day much to our relief she woke up saying 'I've found my sea legs' and the color was back in her face for the first time since we left. She's the love of my life...I can't imagine a day without her.

The night sky and its stars shine brightly; I realise I don't recognize any of them; but of course, they're different than those I knew in Scotland.

Around me the village is quiet and its cottages already dark. Everyone goes to bed early here and I admit I need some sleep too. I hitch a tether line from the wagon to my ankle and settle down on the hard wooden floor. Falling asleep is no problem on my rough bed and I dream I'm back onboard the ship, the sea rocks the deck and the wind blows at my clothes.

I jerk awake then and sit up; my leg is being pulled by the tether line. I jump up to look over the rail and two men are attempting to untie our wagon.

My pulse pounding, I yell "Hey—Get away from there!"

I quickly slip the line off my ankle and leap over the rail, landing solidly on both feet with fists clenched. The men are startled by my quick arrival and both are shorter than me, neither a match. They begin to back away until one pulls the other's arm saying "Come on let's go." They run behind the Church and I continue to hear their feet hit the ground hard, but don't pursue them.

Several of those sleeping inside come at a run after the commotion and find me retying the rope to our wagon; Rose pushes through them.

"Are you alright Daniel?" She asks anxiously.

"Two men were untying our wagon, but they ran behind the Church; probably gone by now." The relief on her face shows as I relate what happened.

Several men run to investigate while the others recheck their own trunks, satisfied to find their belongings untouched.

"We'll take turns on watch until morning," one of them offers, "you go get some sleep. Thanks for standing guard; if you hadn't been out here they'd have taken all our belongings."

I gratefully accept their offer and return inside with Rose to spend the rest of the night on the floor between the pews.

When the sun shines through the eastern window I open my eyes to find Rose looking down from her bed on the pew above me.

"Good morning, my husband." She beams a smile as bright as the sunlight at me. I reach up to stroke her cheek then notice the smell of strong tea brewing. Soon with a cup in hand, it helps me shake off the last of a short night's sleep.

We fold up our blankets and walk to the outhouses behind the Church, returning by the front entrance to check on our trunks again. All appear to be safe, still tied down and untouched after the night's disturbance. We linger to talk with some of the other passengers and wait for James. It's a beautiful, clear day and the town's residents begin to appear on the street.

Some of our shipmates from Scotland soon find us.

"George, good morning. And Mary, hope you slept well last night."

She laughs, "Oh, after months on that ship Daniel, I could have slept on a rock."

"I know what you mean, the pew last night was almost heaven." Rose confirms.

"What are you doing today Daniel?" George asks.

"We have some supplies to take care of; a horse and wagon are first on the list and we'll likely ride out to the farm; How about you?"

"We have a store front leased where we can live upstairs, at least until business builds up. Mary sews and does alterations and I do shoe repair. It'll take a few days to get it ready to open."

"Sounds like something this town could use; we wish you the best." He and I talk of yesterday's events while Rose and Mary talk about whatever women speak of.

"Oh you're so brave Rose, I would have fainted dead away." Mary says and gets her husband's attention.

"George, did you hear what Rose just said? A native on the dock yesterday actually took her hat and gave her a necklace for it."

I turn to Rose in surprise, "You didn't tell me."

"Well I tried Daniel, but you were busy with our trunks. Remember when I said I'd just completed my first trade in New Zealand?" She holds up a green stone talisman to show me from its place around her neck.

"Where did you get that?" James asks as he arrives.

"Hello James, from a native on the dock yesterday. Isn't it pretty?" Rose says.

"Yeah, if you like that stuff I guess. It's hard to get those; what did you trade him?"

"He took my straw hat with the flowers and ribbons on it."

"Boy, are you lucky." He exclaims in envy obviously not placing great value on a woman's straw hat.

"Mom says you should come by for breakfast and she'll fix you a proper meal instead of hard-boiled eggs."

"James, we can't put her to bother, we'll find something here in town." I say as Rose nods in agreement.

"She'll be mad at me if you don't come; she'll think I didn't tell you...you gotta come." James looks down at his shoes so forlornly we agree to follow him to his house.

"Goodbye George, Mary, hope to see you before we head out; if not, good luck. We'll be in town off and on for supplies and we'll look you up to see how you're doing."

"Good Daniel, you're welcome anytime." George assures me.

"Yes, yes, please keep in touch." Mary turns to Rose, "We've come too far together to lose our friendship now."

James and I hitch up the goats to the wagon and we follow him the short distance down the road to his house. He brings the wagon into the fenced front yard

23

and we wait while he gives the goats some water. His mother comes to the doorway then, a young woman about our age, very pretty with red hair smoothed back under a white cap, wearing a clean apron over an everyday dress.

"Hello, so nice to meet you." she calls and holds out her hand. "Jane Ferguson."

"Daniel Smith and this is my wife Rose."

"Come in and please sit down," she invites graciously, "let me take your jacket and shawl. I'll just put them here behind the door."

The one-room wooden cottage is small, built with a clay brick fireplace on the far end. A small shelf along the north wall holds a pitcher and basin with all sorts of cooking pans hung above. Dried flowers and some kind of herbs are overhead on the rafters, their scent is very pleasant. We see the table already set on a white cloth with bowls, cups, spoons, a pot of butter and a blue pitcher of milk and Jane brings a hot pan of porridge from the fireside.

"Help yourselves please."

Our diet on the voyage consisted of some citrus, potatoes, various canned goods, salted beef and at times, some fresh poultry before supplies ran low. Yesterday's meals were small, some biscuits as the ship came up to dock and the leftovers last evening at the Church.

This breakfast is perfect I think as I look at Rose. She smiles and seeing my mouth is already full, she begins to cover for my lack of conversation.

"Thank-you so much for this Jane; how long have you lived here?"

"All my life; I was born on the North Island where dad was a fisherman."

"And do you still have family there?"

"No, my dad died at sea about ten years ago and mum died just last year from consumption."

"I'm so sorry Jane." Rose reaches for her hand.

"They raised me to be strong because it's what you have to be here." Jane continues, "I'm raising James the same way, right?" She tousles his hair and he smiles.

"James' father Jim is a fisherman," she explains. "He stays out for weeks, so I have to be independent and self-sufficient."

"It looks like you've done a fine job with James," I remark as Rose takes a break to eat, "I noticed his worth right away; a good business man and courteous as well. In fact he's agreed to show us around town this morning if it's alright with you?"

"It's perfectly fine Daniel; he can make up his school work this afternoon, right James?"

"Yes Mum." He says a little reluctantly.

"What's this; you don't like school?" Rose asks.

"Well I do except for reading."

"All the more reason to practice, young man" Jane admonishes. "Now you folks come back for lunch, I'll have it waiting when you get done in town."

"Jane, surely you have things you want to do? We can get a meal in town can't we?"

"Oh yes Rose, I'm sure Mrs. Taft has the traps open right now for today's menu."

"Oh no." We both laugh in mock horror then Rose asks, "You're not serious, are you? I've heard rats are a problem near the waterfront."

"I'm just saying, you should come back for lunch." Jane says with a knowing smile.

So we agree to return and leave the loaded goat wagon for Jane to keep an eye on while Rose and I follow James to the blacksmith's shop we passed yesterday on arrival.

The ring of a hammer on iron can be heard as we walk the dusty street and follow its sound to the large, unpainted wooden barn just above the waterfront; its double doors spread wide open.

While Rose waits with James outside, I wander inside to see all the farm tools hanging on the walls and off the rafters. Sunlight peeks through the weathered siding and illuminates chains, plowshares, harnesses of every description, even latch handles for doors and windows. Seemingly, anything done at a forge this smithy can do and I feel lucky he's part of this young town.

The forge burns white hot and orange as he steps on the bellows to fan its coals and sparks blow upward. When finished he plunges the iron piece into a bucket of water where it sizzles, tempers and cools.

The smithy is tall and burly in carriage, his arms muscled and hard from the work. He wears a beat-up leather hat for protection from sparks and a leather apron as well. Heavy leather gloves are pulled off and thrown to the bench beside him as he walks over to greet us.

"Goodday folks... James, what can I do for you?" He smiles at the boy and turns to us, "You're new here aren't you?"

"Yes, Daniel and Rose Smith—off the ship yesterday from Scotland."

"Nice to meet you both; I'm Thomas MacAndrew. You're out for provisions?"

"Mr. MacMillan said to tell you he sent us. We need a wagon and something to pull it, although James here has our trunks loaded on a very good goat wagon."

"Aye, you might need something a little larger but, those goats are strong for their size." He says as he lays a hand on James' shoulder.

"I have two horses at the moment; one a fine rider, the other's been worked hard, but can still carry more than her weight in a cart with no problem. Come on, let's have a look."

I follow him to the back of the building where both horses are stabled. The first, a chestnut gelding, looks about six years old by mouth; his withers are firm and coat shiny.

"How much?" I ask.

"I can let you have him for fifty pounds."

"Will you take twenty-five?"

"Auch man, I can come down a little, within reason; how about forty-five?"

I look at the gelding again then walk to the second horse, a mare seven or eight years old, eyes bright. She stands thin and her coat is dull.

"What's this horse's story?" I ask as I examine her carefully.

"You can see she has one, eh? Found her out on the scrub north of here a few weeks ago; been on her own for some time. She came easily though and appears to have no problem with humans, wears the saddle and reins well."

I look at her mouth then run my hand over her and down her legs. Thomas brings a bridle and I lead her around the paddock to check her gait. Her hooves are healthy but she needs shoes and some care to get back her weight and shiny coat. The way I see it, she's costing him money for upkeep and no one will buy her because of the way she looks.

"Here's what I can do; I'll give you twenty-five pounds for the horse, oats to last two months and shoes all around..." Thomas starts to protest, but I put up my hand to add, "If she fattens up in two months, I'll come in and pay you an additional thirty pounds. It's my final offer and you have my word on it."

"You'll work her, right? Who's to say she'll gain weight?" He asks.

"I have a roof to repair and fences to mend. She won't be at the plow until spring, if she comes back to health. There's a risk she won't, but do you want to continue to take care of her?"

Thomas thinks it over, "You drive a hard bargain." he says and we shake on it.

"Let's go look at the used wagon out back and talk price; You're throwing in the harness with it too, aren't you?" I ask him with an innocent look.

As it turns out, he gives me a good price on the used wagon with tack included. We hitch up the rig after the mare is shod then load the feed.

"Any ideas on where I can purchase a cow and some chickens?"

"You'll pass right by Ethan Shepherd's farm on the way out to your place. He flies a Scot's flag on his house, you can't miss it; tell him I sent you. He had several head of cattle he wanted to sell a couple of weeks ago and he always has chickens. Most sheep come from the north by wagon or boat, but he might sell you some ewes for breeding with his ram."

"Any problem with me just stopping in? Mr. MacMillan said some don't appreciate a stranger on their property."

"Ethan's different, he's been around here a long time and he's used to the occasional stranger. He lost his wife last year and he'll probably appreciate the conversation with you and your wife; he'll give you all the advice you can handle, too."

"I'll need a tarp, maybe ten by twelve, some rope and nails; where can I buy those?"

"I can help with the nails, make em' right here, but the rest would be at Anderson's warehouse down the street. He trades with ships and overland traders from the North Island; keeps a good supply of provisions at honest prices. How many nails you want? I have kegs at six shillings."

"Give me two to start and I'll probably be back next week."

I finish buckling the wagon's harness and help Rose up to the seat before climbing in beside her. James jumps up to ride in the back.

"Thomas, I won't forget how helpful you've been in getting us on the road. If you find yourself out our way, stop on by."

"I just might do it Daniel and thanks for your business." He waves us off and I urge the horse away.

Jane has lunch ready for us when I tie the horse off at the fence and waves as she opens the door, "Come and eat, it's all ready – hope you like fish?"

We sit down at the table and I announce, "James thinks we should name the mare 'Jane."

She laughs, "It would be an honor. I've never had a horse namesake."

When lunch is finished, Daniel and James walk outside to look over the new rig while Jane and I talk.

"When will Jim return?" I ask and sip my tea.

"I expect him soon, they left four weeks ago and usually don't stay longer, but it's hard to say exactly."

"You must miss him. How on earth do you stay occupied while he's gone?"

"Oh my goodness, with James to watch over, there's no problem. The boy's curiosity can get him into all sorts of shenanigans. But he's a good boy and does all he can to fill in during Jim's absence. He helps me around the house, picks up odd jobs and always gives me the money for the house and food. I couldn't ask for a better son."

"That's wonderful. Daniel and I hope to have a family someday."

"We have a good midwife here, she delivered James twelve years ago and she's still going strong. Besides, with the greenstone around your neck, you won't have any problem." She smiles at me and I reach to touch the talisman.

"What do you mean?" I ask.

"It's from the Maori and some say they're fertility tokens. I don't believe in such things, but if you want children, it can't hurt to wear it, can it?"

"Oh my, I had no idea." I reach to take the leather from around my neck. "I'll just put it in my bag until we're ready for its help." We're laughing when Daniel walks in the door.

"If you're ready Rose, we really should go. I don't know what we'll find at the farm and I need to make some sort of shelter for tonight."

"Thanks so much for all you've done, Jane, you've made us feel very welcome here."

"You're both welcome Rose." She picks up a basket from the floor and hands it to me. "Here's some food to get you through the day."

"Oh Jane, you shouldn't have." I say and Daniel moves to bring out a few coins but she stops him.

"Just come visit us when you're in town again, will you? Friends are hard to come by and counting you as such is payment enough."

"Absolutely" I reply and hug her and James before climbing up on the wagon. They wave as Daniel and I drive the mare 'Jane' out to the main road.

"We'll stop at Ethan Shepherd's to see about a cow and some other livestock," Daniel says, "but there isn't time to go for other provisions today. It may be better anyway since we'll know more what we need after we see the place."

I glance down at the basket on the floor and open its lid.

"Daniel, look at this." I find a loaf of home-baked bread, a pot of butter, some homemade jam and two salt-cured ham slices in a canning jar for freshness. "They really are good people."

"Yes. We've met several in these two days and I'm encouraged and very grateful for that."

We find Ethan's house about halfway to our farm; the Scot's flag flies from his porch and I turn our rig into the dirt lane. The house is a white-washed clapboard, a little larger than those along the way. His farmland is well-kept with neat fences winding out over the gentle slopes to outline several fields full of sheep. A couple of cows graze by the barn as we pull up and several chickens scratch and cluck in the yard.

"Hello." A hearty voice calls from the house. "State your business and we'll see if I'll come out to greet you."

I'm a little startled at the demand but nevertheless remember what Mr. MacMillan said, so I climb down from the wagon and stand facing the house.

"I'm Daniel Smith and this is my wife Rose. We've rented the old farm down the road and Thomas MacAndrew sent us by. He said you might have some stock you'd sell."

We hear a lock come off the front door and a gentleman perhaps in his early forties dressed in work clothes steps outside, his hair a curly brown and face tanned.

"All you had to say. Thomas is a good man and anyone he sends is good enough for me." He reaches to shake my hand and touches the brim of his hat to Rose.

"Come in Daniel," he invites, "We'll sit a little, have some tea and see what we can come up with." He helps Rose down from the wagon.

"I appreciate your hospitality Mr. Shepherd and tea sounds good. We do need to get to the farm before too long though, so I can build some sort of shelter for the night."

"Call me Ethan." We follow him across the wide porch and through the front door. The house is larger than either of us expected from the outside. The great room before us has a large stone fireplace to the right and spacious kitchen to the left. The long row of windows on the back wall looks out over his fields as they rise and fall down to the harbor. Several large cushioned chairs and an oversize settee make the room look comfortable.

"What a wonderful view." Rose exclaims and walks over to enjoy the wide vista.

"Yes, my wife always wanted windows when we started out in our cabin, so when we built this bigger house I had them brought down from Auckland; our 'windows on the world' she called them."

"How long have you been in New Zealand?" I ask.

35

"Daniel, I came on a trade ship to the North Island in 1828; stayed at Wellington for several years and met my Catherine; seems like just yesterday." He adds. "We decided to move down when the Maori started their infighting. When we saw the harbor, we knew we wanted to stay here."

He turns away from the window to walk to the kitchen, a strong-looking man despite a slight limp. "Sit down and I'll get the tea and some bread and jam. Got in on the ship yesterday, did you?"

"Yes, we stayed at the Church last night. Didn't get a lot of sleep though; two men tried to steal our wagon."

"You don't say. I hate to hear of it, but unfortunately with the ships' trade and crews who come ashore, you never know what to expect. Those living here are good people; it's the drifters who cause trouble looking for something they don't have to work for."

"Do you hear of it often?" Rose asks as she watches him put slices of cold meat on a plate.

"Not often, but it has occurred. Used to be the Maori's were our only problem; always wanting to take what they thought was theirs off the land. You see they believe the land will always be theirs and the people living on it are their tenants. The fights between tribes

36

in the North over land boundaries became so serious the British had to come in to protect the settlers. You probably heard didn't you Daniel?"

"We heard some news of it in Scotland but thought a treaty settled it."

"It would have, had the treaty been honored but it didn't take long for them to realise it was useless. Things still aren't good up there, but here we have peace and hope it stays." Ethan brings the pot of tea to the table, along with bread and the cold meat sliced thin. "Hope you like this, it's pickled pork from a recipe my Catherine used to make."

"It looks delicious Ethan" Rose responds.

He turns to me, "One word of caution and we'll get to the livestock. Do you have a gun Daniel?"

"I have a rifle for hunting."

He walks over to a cabinet in the corner of the room and unlocks its door to take out a Colt Paterson pistol. "This gun has been a good friend to me since I started out here," he pauses to look down the barrel, "I'd like to give it to you Daniel, it might be useful someday."

"Ethan, I can't accept it, it's too valuable."

"Go on, take it." he says as he puts the gun and two boxes of ball ammunition with a full powder horn into a burlap bag. "I traded some stock for it. The man who owned it came from the States and fought in the

Comanche wars in Texas. I get no use out of it anymore and you'll need it until you get established and known. This is still a wild country and full of surprises; you need to be prepared, Daniel."

Rose doesn't hold with guns I think as I accept the bag and lay it out of her sight on the floor. But I realise his advice is right and I'll take the gun with us. We need to get the farm restored for spring in September. Anyone who tries to prevent it or threatens us, will be on the wrong end of the pistol and I'll have no choice but to defend my family.

Ethan picks up his tea then focuses on its china cup and finds himself thinking of Catherine.

She chose these dishes long ago; things around here constantly remind me of her. Regret lingers in my gut, a miserable thing and once again I admonish myself; perhaps she'd still be here if I'd made different decisions. I look up to watch Daniel put the burlap bag on the floor while Rose looks first at him, then me.

I won't let either of them know any of this; they'll learn their own lessons and I pray both their lives will be long and prosperous.

Chapter 2 Friendship

"I think you two should stay here for the night," Ethan offers, "and get a fresh start in the morning. What do you think Daniel?"

I glance out the window, the afternoon is late and shadows are lengthening.

Weariness still shows on my Rose's face from our months at sea and the dark circles under her eyes haven't changed with last night's sleep on a hard pew.

"Ethan, we don't want to inconvenience you, but I'd be wrong to refuse your hospitality if you're serious."

"You folks take my big bed," he orders, "I just put clean sheets on this morning. I still keep up the housekeeping; my Catherine, she'd be mighty upset if I didn't.

"I'll turn in on the divan in my office and tomorrow we can take a look at what stock I have left and see if you're interested."

He seems genuinely excited about our company.

"We're both very grateful for your hospitality Ethan." I put my arm around Rose's shoulders to pull her up from the comfort of the settee.

"You're very welcome Daniel. Now, I remember my Catherine's habits very well and she always wanted to bathe before bed. The tub is already in the room, towels in the washstand, the cook stove's still burning and the bucket is out by the pump.

"You can fetch the water and it'll be hot in no time – I reckon life onboard ship didn't allow for too many tub baths."

He laughs and we both agree it certainly hadn't.

"I'm out to the barn to put the animals to bed and check their water. I like to wander my farm a little in the cool of evening and clear the day from my head before bed."

He grabs his jacket and hat and walks toward the back door, "See you folks in the morning."

I cool a bucket of hot water with a bucket of well water and let Rose have the first soak while I follow Ethan's example and take a walk outside, too.

The moon is full and reminds me of the moonlight over Scotland's moors. Walking those fields as a lad, I had no idea one day I'd be in a strange country far from home.

This moon isn't even visible at home now I think, separated as we are by time and miles. At the barn, I look out over the sloping hills and down to the harbor.

Memories of my homeland and the past come again and I recall my work at the quarry. How thrilling it was to see a big slab of granite split away and shake the ground when it fell.

I'd planned to learn from the ground up and someday run an operation of my own but the economy continued downward and I became part of the layoff.

Odd jobs laying granite setts on roadways earned a meager living after that. We even delayed starting a family and thought better times would come but we had to move in with my parents just to survive.

When I saw the poster from the New Zealand Company, it made something turn over inside and I thought *here is hope*, something we can actually do to make our life better.

We left little behind, selling everything we owned for stake money to sustain us through the first year.

Rose was afraid to leave at first but she finally accepted the truth; everyone around us had entered hard times for the long run.

My parents insisted we take a small gift and though I knew they could have used it for themselves, we honored them by accepting. I still feel the shame of a grown man accepting their charity.

Now I look out over the valley and harbor below as the moon lights it up in a wash of soft light. Clouds hang illuminated along the horizon and stars against the darkness appear unusually close.

We're actually here I think and reality at last begins to set in.

Ethan joins me, "Beautiful isn't it?"

Then he says in a low voice, "Come over here and look at something, but be quiet."

I follow him until he stops to point down one of the fence lines.

A small group of men moves around the grazing field, the last hoists something white to his shoulder...a sheep. Then they turn north and walk into the woods.

"Who are they?" I ask.

"Maori natives, out for their regular share of what belongs to them." Ethan answers.

"What are you talking about? Should we go after them?"

"No, not necessary; we've had an unwritten agreement for years. They show up about every three months and collect one sheep I leave for them in the east pasture. In return, they don't bother the rest of my stock or the house."

"I don't understand, what happens if you stop?"

"I sell this farm or worse, it causes a land war with them none of us is equipped to fight or stop.

"No, I have no problem with a small amount of my profit shared in the form of an occasional sheep. So far they've been honorable in their side of the deal and I'll continue to ride it out unless things change."

"What could change?"

"If relations get too hot between the settlement and the Maori, we'll find ourselves overrun with British soldiers on behalf of the Queen Mother to preserve peace.

"It means either fight the Maori until they move on to other parts of the country, or they're wiped out. They aren't easy to deal with, but they don't deserve to lose everything they believe they were given by their Gods.

"I choose the high road and share what I can with them, so far it's worked." He's silent for a moment.

"Will I be expected to do the same? I won't see profit anytime soon." I ask.

"I think the time will come when you do see them at your farm.

"They speak our language, enough to communicate; some were trained by the early missionaries, but reading is another matter.

"They'll know you're new to the area, best thing you can do is appear strong and wise, but don't get tricked into a fight. Some love to prove who's the strongest and believe it should be their warrior at any cost."

Ethan continues as he leans against the fence post beside me. "These natives were flesh eaters of their enemies in early days and I don't trust them even at this late date.

"Some are more antagonistic than others, especially between tribes in the North. They've learned the whites' agreements and pakeha as we're called can't be trusted. The land is sacred to them and they've lost much. I decided to move here because most live in peace."

"What else should I know you're not telling me?"

"You have a rifle and a pistol; find a good place to hide them both; someplace you can still get to them when needed, but where no one else would think to look.

"They want guns to fight rival tribes and at times, against the British in the north. You'll know when the time comes to use the gun as a threat or to kill, but until then, keep it safe from theft. Some have no problem going into open houses and barns to help themselves to whatever they like."

I walk back to the house with him and say good night. Rose is sound asleep when I enter the bedroom, so I quietly undress and sit down in the now cold water of the tub.

It suits my mood and chills me no more than the stories Ethan just told me. I fight down panic and feel a terrible responsibility for bringing Rose so far to face a wild and dangerous land. Hardship we both expected, but natives who think they can walk into our home at any time are another matter.

The posters in Scotland were misleading and I fell for their 'paradise' descriptions.

By the time I dry off, the moonlight has disappeared behind clouds. I silently slip into bed and fall into a sound sleep, safe behind Ethan's locked doors, if only for tonight. Tomorrow is a new day.

Morning dawns and we awake to the smell of bacon.

"Are we in heaven?" Rose asks sleepily.

"I think Ethan must be cooking." I proceed to climb over the edge of the feather bed to get dressed but Rose holds me back with a touch and caress, persuading me to linger a little longer in the warmth of her arms.

Later I throw off the covers, "You take your time Rose; I'll go out and see if I can help with chores."

"Morning, Daniel." Ethan calls from his post at the stove. "You two get some sleep last night?"

"We did, thanks to you Ethan. I don't think it would have gone half as well at the farm."

"Why?"

"Well, Mr. MacMillan said the roof 'needed some thatch' and the furniture would 'probably' be dried out by now from the rainy season; not exactly encouragement for a good night's sleep."

"Well, don't worry, it'll all straighten out. In the meantime, sit yourself down to a good breakfast. Morning, Rose." Ethan says as she enters looking refreshed and rested.

"My-oh-my," Ethan exclaims, "certainly nice to have a woman in the house again." He pulls out a chair for her.

"Why thank you Ethan. I came out to help you with breakfast but you've already done all the work, this is lovely."

The table is set with china; rashers of bacon and sliced bread placed in the center. Bowls for porridge, a dish of butter and a pitcher of milk complete the welcome setting.

"It's my pleasure." He sits down to ask God's blessing on 'my two young guests and their new farm' in addition to the food.

"You know what I'm thinking Daniel?" he asks as he starts to eat, "I'm between chores here, sold a lot of my stock except for a few cows, sheep and chickens. What if I come out to the farm with you and see if I can do anything to help get it into shape?"

I look at Rose for a moment then answer, "A proud man would refuse your offer, but I'm not a fool.

"From the looks of your farm, you're very good at what you do. I'm starting from scratch with a lot to learn, so even your opinion on how to proceed would be good as gold. I'll take you up on your generous offer."

"Good." Ethan replies and seems to eat a little faster as we plan what to take out to the farm.

Later while Rose clears the table, I carry out the bath water then walk to the barn with Ethan to hitch up the horses to both wagons.

∽∽∽

While the men are still at the barn, I finish up the dishes and put them away then repack a few things taken off the wagon for the night and tidy the bed.

Glancing around the room, I notice a woman's tintype picture on the dresser. She must be Ethan's wife I think and pick up it up for a closer look.

She sits on a beautiful horse about eight hands high, her light-colored hair stuffed up into a broad-brimmed hat and the farmland behind her. I wonder what she died of so young, but I don't want to be intrusive.

If something happened to Daniel, what would I do? Better not to think of such things, I quickly decide. I've always believed we leave the earth in the Lord's own time and it's no matter where we are; no use to worry when or how I resolve.

I grab my valise and carry it out to the wagon where Daniel and Ethan stand talking by the hitching post.

I overhear the word 'Maori', but they stop when they see me.

"All ready?" Ethan asks.

I answer, "Sure am."

"Alright, let's get started; shouldn't take more than an hour out to your place."

He locks the doors on the house then climbs onto his rig to lead the way out.

Before we reach the farm, we stop to water the horses at a quiet stream flowing down from the mountains and across the road. Its water is crystal clear, shallow and easily crossed, but Ethan warns it becomes swift and wider in the rainy season.

"If it happens, you may as well turn around and wait another day, it's not worth the risk of crossing."

While Daniel stays with the horses, I walk over to Ethan where he leans against a beech tree.

"I couldn't help but notice the lovely picture on the dresser in your room. It's Catherine isn't it?"

"Yes, she was as beautiful as the day is long, my partner in work and my joy in life. It's been hard losing her." He continues to look across the stream.

"I can only imagine and am so sorry for your loss. It's a lovely picture, how in the world did you obtain it?"

"It's quite a story," he pulls back from his thoughts to look at me.

"One day a gentleman knocked at our door after we built the house, said he was a photographer and asked if he could take our picture with the big box he carried on his rig.

"We looked at each other and said 'sure, why not.' He'd traveled all over the colonies taking pictures of the land and people for some book he wanted to write about settlers.

"Before he left, he gave us two pictures; one of Catherine on her horse and one of us together."

"How wonderful to have such a thing." I exclaim.

49

"Yes, it's both a blessing and a reminder of what's missed; but I find as time passes, I grow more appreciative because it keeps her image alive for me. I'll always remember her, no matter how many years separate us."

He comes away from the tree then, "You ready to see your new home?"

We take the wagons a short distance from the stream to a rise in the road and spot the little gray stone cottage right where the map indicates.

However, Mr. MacMillan's description lacked some serious detail.

The house sits completely taken over by vines and weeds right up to the tops of its stone walls. "Roof" does not describe the reality, as nothing of the original roof remains, not even its beams.

Rose and I stand in front of the long-deserted cottage and wonder where to start. This will not be something we can do in a day, week, or month I think to myself.

Ethan works at cutting a path to the door with a big knife but when I put the key into the rusty lock, it won't turn.

We both put our shoulders into it and push it right over, the rotten frame falls easily from the stonework into the house.

"It wouldn't have held anyway." Ethan remarks and squints at the mess inside.

Leftover furniture lays upside down, broken and rotted from exposure to the elements over the years.

A few dishes survive on a shelf beside an oil lantern and a small mirror hangs beside the door with a faded painting of a man and woman next to it.

Rose moves to go in, but I stop her until we have a chance to enter and make sure it's safe.

Ethan says there are no snakes in this country, but some insects are unpleasant to encounter, including a poisonous spider, though he doubts any would be this far from the harbor.

When we finally call Rose in, she stands still at first then begins to look around.

∝و৻ও

I examine the small mirror then study the painting; "Daniel, I wonder if these were the first owners?"

The stone fireplace is comforting with its solid appearance amid the general chaos of the space and I feel grateful it will provide us a safe fire in the colder months.

The walls look high enough to make a loft for our bed and though the little cottage is a mess now, it has possibilities.

"It's not that bad" I say and smile at Daniel's worried face. "We can make this a really nice home, it has possibilities."

"You heard the lady," Ethan says, "It's not that bad."

Daniel looks at us both and starts laughing.

"It's not that bad." he repeats and we all start laughing at the sheer absurdity of it.

"It's so bad its downright insane." he adds and we continue until tears run down our cheeks.

After we regain control, the men walk outside to start a list of supplies needed now and later. Laughter can do miracles I think and begin to pull out items which can't be salvaged to a burn pile in the yard.

When finished, the only thing worth saving is a small washstand. I keep it as our first official piece of furniture and place the little painting, the mirror and a few of the intact dishes inside the cabinet.

Next I retrieve a bucket from the wagon and start to clean out the fireplace debris. When I look inside the chimney though, I can't see daylight - not a good sign.

"Daniel, can you come here for a moment?" I call to him outside. He pokes his head around the doorway.

"What's wrong Rose?"

"I think the chimney's blocked up with vines or something, I can't see daylight."

She comes to drop a kiss on my cheek in her elation over the house, my wife the eternal optimist I think.

"I'll go take a look down the top." I tell her then return outside to scale the stone chimney and look inside.

"We have half a tree in here." I call to Ethan who comes to help me clear the heavy vines blocking the chimney's top and we pull the dead tree limb out.

Ethan comments, "It must have blown in from a storm." I return back inside to peer up the chimney.

It's clear, but the damper is completely rusted out. Without replacing it, our heat will go straight up the chimney and I add a visit to Thomas at his blacksmith shop to the list.

Ethan takes a shovel and bucket to scoop up dirt, wood, scraps of broken furniture and carries it all outside to the burn-pile. Rose is thrilled to see the stone floor at last.

"No place for bugs to get in here, I feel better already." She declares.

"Ethan, I'm worried about a water supply."

"I noticed too, Daniel; maybe an old well outback somewhere?"

We walk around the back of the house, hacking our way through thick vegetation.

Ethan points out some plants to me; "Matagouri and Prickly Spaniard, see these thorns? Both are too sharp to be in a pasture around livestock." He shows me two more plants called ragwort and tutu; "These are poisonous." The look on his face is serious.

"Looks like we have a lot of work clearing this stuff before putting any livestock in," I reply, "I'm rapidly having doubts about our spring deadline."

"Don't worry Daniel; we may need to hire some help from the settlement for a week or so, but a lot of this stuff can be burned off too.

"Most isn't anything but an inconvenience to livestock, Tea Tree and Black Scrub like these" he points out, "can stay until we get to it."

We stumble onto some old wood from ruins of a barn and a dogleg fence. Just in front of it, we discover a rusty watering trough covered by weeds and sure enough, an old wellhead next to it with no pump.

"What do you think? Does the well have water?" I ask Ethan.

"Your guess is as good as mine. Only way to tell is put a pole down inside or bring a hand pump and some water to prime it.

"Afternoon's about gone; what do you say we head back to my place, sit down to some supper and figure out our next move?" He asks.

"Sounds good to me, but we'll have to rent a room at this rate."

"You should know better, there's room aplenty at the house as long as you need it." Ethan insists, "besides, this is more fun than I've seen in a long time and I'm enjoying it."

We hitch up and make it back to the house by sunset. While Ethan and I take care of the horses, Rose goes on into the house and assures us she is cooking tonight.

❧❧

After I change into a clean dress and wash off the dust of the day, I'm ready to fix something for supper, but what?

I remember Jane's salt-cured ham stored in Ethan's cool cellar and find some beans in the kitchen cabinet. When the men come in from the barn, I'll ask Ethan if it'd be alright to make some soup.

55

"Rose, I haven't had a home-cooked meal in months." He replies, "If you make the soup, I'll go get some carrots out of the garden."

I laugh at his enthusiasm and put the big pot of water and beans to boil.

He returns with some carrots and onions so I peel and add them all to the beans and ham which already simmer. Later, I'll bake some biscuits on top of the stove in an iron fry pan since I haven't yet mastered the oven.

The meal is a success to my satisfaction and I sit back to enjoy a cup of tea while the men discuss the next day's plan.

"I think the well and the roof are first priority," Daniel says, "with maybe the damper for the fireplace next. What do you think?"

"You're right about the well; if the water's bad or just isn't there, we'll need to get a diviner out to find you a new one. Once the water's available, you'll be able to sustain life, yours and the livestock.

"I'll tell you something else," he continues. "If it were me, I'd be having some words with MacMillan about the first month's rent you gave him.

"If he wants the rental property returned to its workable condition, he should be paying you. I also think you'd be within your rights to request a new contract stating the rent will not go up after the place is restored."

"Do you think it a possibility?" Daniel asks.

"I've known Charles a long time and I believe he's an honest man, but he's a Company man and takes his orders from the main Office. Still, it wouldn't hurt to sit down with him and talk the situation over."

"I need to go in tomorrow and pick up a hand pump and new watering trough," Daniel says, "I'll stop at the Land Office, too. Who does water divining?"

"It's been a while but I think Thomas may know since people come to him for the rods. I'll go along with my wagon and pick up some supplies, too." Ethan adds then rises from his chair to leave on his nightly rounds outside.

"See you folks early so we can get on the road."

"We certainly owe Ethan a debt of gratitude." Rose remarks as she clears the table.

"It's a fact." She doesn't know just how much I think as the warnings he gave me last night remain in my mind.

∾༄

This morning we eat eggs, porridge and the last of the biscuits from last evening's supper. The sun's first rays come over the crest as we start on the road into town. We take both wagons to Thomas's where we find him already at the forge.

"Ethan!" He comes over to shake hands. "I haven't seen you in months. How are you?"

Ethan grips his hand hard and replies "Doing better and have some visitors, you know Daniel and Rose I believe?"

"I do indeed. Daniel, how's the farm?"

We all look at each other speechless and fail to answer his question.

"It's that good, eh?" Thomas responds to our hesitation and we share some of what we're up against.

"Sorry to hear it. The last I passed by, the Riley's lived there. They had a sweet little spread, but moved close to town as they got older and sold to the Land Company, must be about six years now."

"We found a small painting, it must be them." Rose adds, "I wonder why they left it."

"Sometimes people leave things to remind those who come after of a place's history. The Riley's were some of the first to settle here and proud of what they had. Both are gone and I reckon the picture is history now."

"Thomas, do you think you could fabricate a new damper for our fireplace, the old one is rusted out."

"Sure, provided the measurements are accurate and the chimney's square, you know Daniel, sometimes numbers can throw a person. Once I do the work the bill is due whether it fits or not." he cautions in fairness.

"Understood; do you ever go out to have a look for yourself, I mean can you add a little to the price to see it done right?"

"Well if you're willing to reimburse me, say for two hours travel time, I can."

"Consider it a deal then. When can you come?"

"Is tomorrow morning too soon? I'll bring my rods and see what we can find in the way of a well too, if you'd like."

The plan set for the following day, we go on to the Land Office to speak with Mr. MacMillan, as Ethan suggested.

Charles MacMillan greets us more calmly than the previous day and invites us all to take a seat. He assures us he has spare time since his last new resident came last evening.

"What can I do for you?"

"Mr. MacMillan, there's been some sort of mistake."

"Oh? What do you mean, Daniel?"

"Well, you represented the farmhouse would be easily put in working order and only needed some roof work and a new bed.

"Instead what we've rented is a roofless house, no well, no furniture and a fireplace needing work. There won't be any farming until a barn can be built and the fences set, with all of these things repaired or replaced and made livable." I take a breath and ask the question point-blank.

"What do you intend to do about it Mr. MacMillan?"

"Oh my, I wasn't aware...I had no idea the place lay in such disrepair. I'm not sure what I can do but refund your first month's rent. Of course it would mean you couldn't stay in the house." he finishes weakly.

"Mr. MacMillan, in its present condition, unless we lived in a tent, there is no shelter in the house. We've come a long way at your personal and professional promise a workable farm would be ready."

I get up from my chair to walk around the end of the desk and look at him eye-to-eye.

"I do have a proposal which might benefit us both. You pay me for materials and labor to rebuild the roof as well as a small barn shelter for feed and the like and, to get a new well in.

"I'd like a new contract at the same rent, with option to buy the fifty acres and buildings at the end of ten years or before; market value not to exceed £40 per acre. If we agree, we'll call this problem solved." I conclude and wait to hear his answer.

Mr. MacMillan takes a few minutes to consider my suggestions. His job depends on producing profit for the Company in land sales and happy immigrants encourage further land sales so I'm hopeful he'll work with me.

I also know from what Ethan tells me, the New Zealand Company isn't interested in rental property anymore. A proposal for an option to buy might get the main office's attention since, in its present condition, there's no way to garner income from it.

"Very well Mr. Smith," MacMillan says finally, "I understand and share your alarm at the farm's condition, especially with the approach of winter in a few months.

"Your proposal sounds fair, however I'll need to get final approval from the main office and I need a written estimate of the cost plus labor from you.

"In the meantime, I'll refund your first month's rent but hold you to the existing contract until I get approval from the Wellington office for the new one. If you'd care to take a seat, we can work out the details and you can write an estimate sheet to go with it."

"Sounds good Mr. MacMillan and I'm pleased to work with you."

Smiling for the first time since arriving, I ask Ethan, "You mind staying to advise me on cost of materials and questions on the labor? You know more about the area than I do."

"Sure, don't mind at all." He answers.

"Daniel, I'll just walk down to Jane's to see if she's home." Rose says, "No use in my staying, just pick me up when you're finished."

"Alright" I answer then turn back to Mr. McMillan and the matter at hand.

❧❧

When I step out onto the dusty wooden walk in front of the office, it feels good to walk in a town again and I turn down the street toward Jane's.

Mary Strickland is just down the street in front of her storefront and waves to me.

"Rose." she calls out and I walk toward her.

"It's so good to see you. How are you; are you settled in? Come into the shop and we can sit a while." She says.

"I really can only stay a moment; Daniel and I will be meeting somewhere else. So this is your new shop – it's perfect." I look at the tiny, wood-framed building with a large glass window fronting on the main street.

"Yes, it's hard to see it as we plan, but come in and I'll show you."

"Just for a minute." and I follow her up the dusty front steps.

"Now the counter will be here, chairs over here and fitting rooms in this area. George's shoe business will be in the back, accessible from the back door and we'll share the front window with our wares. I've decided to offer custom hats for women too."

"It's wonderful Mary, I'm so happy for you and George. We're staying with a friend until the farmhouse can be repaired, but as soon as we move in we'll have you both out for a good visit."

"We'd love to; you stop by again when we can visit a while."

"I will; goodbye." I continue to walk to Jane's but look back over my shoulder at Mary who is again on the sidewalk, concentrating happily on her front window.

I pass the Church on the way to Jane's but when I glance up its steps, she's coming down them.

"Jane." I wave but she acts strangely, almost as if she's been crying.

"Jane, are you okay?"

"Oh Rose, Jim isn't home yet and I'm worried sick." She breaks down then and I help her sit down on the bottom step.

"There, there, I'm sure he's fine Jane. Surely he's been late before?"

"Yes, but never more than four weeks and it's been almost five weeks now." She makes an effort to mop up her tears with her apron and straighten her cap which has gone askew.

"I'm just being silly I guess, but I came here to say a prayer and talk to Pastor Bush."

"Never a bad time to say a prayer and I know it will bring comfort to you." I tell her, "Try not to worry, let's walk back to your house. Daniel's picking me up when he's finished in town."

We talk and she seems calmer when we reach the cottage. James sits out front with his goats.

"Hello Mam, come for a visit?"

"Just a quick one until Daniel comes to pick me up."

"Come inside, I'll get you some water and we can catch up." Jane says.

I tell her of the previous day at the farm and about Ethan who has been such a blessing. Jane hasn't met him but heard of his wife's death last year.

"Do you know how she died?" I ask.

"I think she fell from her horse and hit her head on a rock out in the pasture. By the time he found her, she was dead."

"How tragic for him." I am stunned as I imagine the tragedy.

"Yes; he doesn't come into town much anymore, so I'm surprised he's had you two stay."

"I think we were something of a blessing to him, as he's been to us; he's changed in just these few days. Odd how things work out isn't it?"

"It is, like how I really needed your visit today to lift my spirits." Jane says with a smile.

"Can we do anything for you while we're here?" I ask her.

"Oh goodness no, I have my little man James and stores set by. As long as fish are in the harbor, we'll have food to eat. James will pick up some odd jobs so don't worry. I've been doing this for a long time and we'll be fine. Now, what can I do for you?"

"You can tell me the best place to get some fish for tonight's supper." I reply.

"James – come take Rose's order for some fish." He comes quickly in the door at her call and I suspect he's been listening all along.

"What kind would you like and how big?" We laugh at his confidence as he leaves for the harbor.

Daniel arrives a little later to take me along to Anderson's warehouse where we fill both wagons to capacity with roofing supplies, the new hand pump and a watering trough. I'm amazed at the variety of inventory Mr. Anderson carries and realise he is charged with keeping settlers supplied through the four seasons.

When we return to Jane's, Daniel introduces Ethan to her and tells him how she rescued us from the "soup restaurant." Then James comes back with two large salmon and packs them in the bottom of the new water trough for the trip back. We say our goodbyes but I am a little worried about Jane's situation.

By five o'clock I've cooked up several thick steaks of salmon and salted down the remainder to keep for later. We sit down to eat the fish with fried potatoes, fresh from Ethan's garden. The men linger at the table to plan for the return to the farm tomorrow and while I clean up the kitchen and listen to them, I realise I want to be a part of this.

"I'd like to go too if it's alright Daniel. I'll take a broom to the farmhouse floor and maybe clean out more weeds in the yard."

"Of course, if you don't think you'll be bored? We have work in the field to do."

"I'll be fine Daniel, let me feather my nest while you two are busy."

"I have an extra broom in the barn, you're welcome to it." Ethan offers. I know he bought it today intentionally for us and I look at him, but he doesn't let on.

"It's very generous of you." I take the offered broom, knowing he'll be hurt if I don't; later I add it to my stack for the wagon in the morning.

The next day dawns and we roll the wagons, stopping at the stream again on the way. The water runs clear and sweet and the horses drink while we fill our cups and a water bottle for the day.

"Sure wish this ran through our place" Daniel says.

"Well, in a manner of speaking, it does," Ethan replies. "If you head to the north end of your property, this creek runs across the corner of your land. You'll be able to dig a nice pond for your sheep, but it's far enough away from the house so you won't get any flooding."

"It's about time we got some good news about the farm for a change." Daniel remarks and Ethan smiles at us in agreement.

Chapter 3 Changes

*E*than and I tie off the mare Jane at the front of the house and take his rig to the back while Rose goes inside with her bucket and broom to begin clearing the floor.

Out at the well, Ethan accesses the clay pipe of the old well shaft by pushing a sapling pole down inside to feel for any blockage or breaks. The pole's tip comes back moist from the bottom and we hope it's a good sign.

"What do you think Ethan?"

"Couldn't hurt to try it, but I'm not promising anything." We connect the pump and take turns priming it with buckets of water brought from the stream.

"Average depth of water in this area is about thirty feet, but with the stream so close by it may be less." Ethan says. He puts his ear to the pipe but hears no sign our work is successful.

"Appears this well is nothing but dry, Daniel." He wipes the sweat from his forehead, "It's damp at the bottom, so it might need to go deeper but I suggest it be moved further from the barn anyway."

We take a breather; ironically the stream water is refreshing and quenches our thirst so we sit down on the buckets to rest and stare at the new pump sitting useless in front of us.

"This is a fine scene – are you willing the water out of the ground?" spouts Thomas as he walks with Rose from the front of the house.

"He came by horse and near startled me to death." she says with a smile.

"No good news here I'm afraid, the well may be over water but we can't pump it." Ethan says.

"There is some mud on the gauge stick though." I add.

"Let's find you some water." Thomas says and takes out two iron rods from a sack. "If it was down there once, it'll be around here someplace."

He takes a bent rod in either hand, braces his elbows at his sides and points the rods straight ahead of him as he walks slow and steady from the old well head straight out to the pasture.

At about forty feet, the rods swing mysteriously in toward each other and Thomas yells "Aha."

He marks the spot with a rock, turns the rods straight out again and walks to his right. Within ten feet, the rods turn into each other again.

After marking the place, he walks halfway between the two markers. I watch with amazement as he turns sideways and side-steps parallel between the two for a couple of feet.

The rods turn outward and point away from each other and he lays a stone down again.

"You've got water under the ground from the northeast corner of your spread and it should be between those markers. Don't ask me how I can be sure; I can't tell you how deep to dig, but it's there – the rods don't lie."

I clap him on the back with enthusiasm. Rose will soon get her wish to scrub her house clean I think to myself.

"Thomas, I've heard they can drill a well with an auger bit now and a couple of horses; know where we can get one of those?"

"You're in luck, I just acquired one in a recent trade – only thing is I'd like to see it used and I can't get out here again for several days. You have any trouble with a few days wait?"

"I'm not put off by the delay and have many things to do in the meantime. A week from Friday would be fine."

"Good. I want to see this "drilling" for water so I can offer the service to the new settlers. We'll need clay tiles from Anderson's to line the well and we'll also need a piece of solid hardwood to cap it off, predrilled for the pump access of course." Thomas finishes.

"I'll bring the wood." Ethan volunteers.

Thomas draws up some rough plans for the framework to hold the auger.

"Pray we don't hit any bedrock layers before the water." he adds.

"Now – how about I measure your firebox and chimney and get back to the shop."

❧

"Rose, I need to take some measurements in here, okay if I come in?" Thomas calls to me from the doorway.

'In' is a relative matter at this point." I joke. "Of course, please come in and make yourself at home Thom."

He measures the fireplace while I finish up all I can do with a broom until the roof is built.

I long to start scrubbing away the grime built up from years of rain and open air. I even took window sizes for future curtains after cutting away the vines from the open windows

We're a long way from 'curtain-ready' but someday, I think and wander off into dreams of my own for our house.

Thomas walks by, "See you next week Rose, I'll be back to help with the well drilling."

"See you then Thomas."

Picking up some gloves, I am ready to see what can be done in the front yard.

∽👁∾

Out in the woods, Ethan and I finish cutting young timber for the drill framework, a sturdy tripod frame which will support the auger shaft and the attached arms connected to the horse's collar.

The mare Jane will walk round and round and if all goes well, the auger will cut through the thirty to forty feet of earth to find our new water.

"You know if this doesn't work, you have a stream across your property." Ethan says as we load the poles into the wagon.

"It wouldn't be easy, but you could bring it back by wagon every two or three days for what you need in the house and for small animals, chickens and the like."

"You're right of course Ethan. I know I should be grateful for what we have, it's just...we have a vision of what it should be like, you know?"

"It was the same with me when we started building our farm. We worked ourselves hard for what we have today." Ethan stops to look at me.

"It cost us years of precious time and ultimately Catharine her life. Just keep track of where you're at Daniel; perfection isn't everything in this world and things which matter most are usually right by your side. Enjoy your dreams and your life with Rose along the way."

He smiles at me and I think he probably sees a younger version of himself; I'll remember his advice.

When we bring the wood to the house, we're amazed to see Rose has singlehandedly cleared most of the front yard. She sits on one of the buckets by the doorway waiting for us.

"I can't believe how much you've accomplished without us." I tell her.

"You two aren't the only ones working around here you know." she says with pride.

We leave the roofing supplies in the wagon, "No use taking chances on someone helping themselves." Ethan tells me, "We'll bring it back home for now."

After a rest we eat some bread and honey then hitch up the wagons for the trip back to Ethan's.

It's been a long and work-filled day; each of us feels grateful for what we've accomplished. After supper, we make it an early night.

In a week's time, we succeed in setting up the auger Thomas brought to us and with a couple of setbacks and corrections of the framework, we make good time with the actual drilling.

At thirty-five feet, we find water with only one extension added to the auger's length. Luckily, Thomas already received instructions on lining the well from the man he traded with and we finish it off with the tiles.

By dropping a small tin cup down the shaft on a rope, a cold, somewhat muddy sample of water is brought up. It's sweet and we all sample it for luck.

The well is capped off with the thick slab of wood Ethan brought from his farm and I mount the pump to prime it.

"You ready Daniel?" Ethan asks me with a funny look, then winks and nods toward Thomas who doesn't notice.

"Would you pump the first bucket Thomas?" Ethan asks.

"Not at all, it would be an honor." Thomas proceeds to pump the handle briskly until we hear the gurgling up the shaft and a splash of water hits the bucket.

"There she is." I declare happily. Rose cheers and Thomas continues to pump a full bucket.

I follow Ethan's lead and help him pick it up then unceremoniously dump its entire icy contents over Thomas's head before he realises what's happening.

"Welcome to the well drilling business, Mate." Ethan says as we dodge away with Thomas chasing after us. He soon stops his attack to sputter and shake his hair like a wet spaniel.

"Well, thanks; I guess it's an honor." He's smiling as he says it so we're forgiven and Rose goes to fetch a towel.

Our daily trips to the stream for water are at an end, making the garden much easier to maintain. Rose planted a kitchen garden with carrots and yams, root vegetables which Ethan says will do well, even into the first weeks of winter.

We began the roof this week after I abandoned my first plan to use thatch for some unclaimed slate at Anderson's. Traded off a ship from Auckland, the lot wasn't enough for a government building, but will be plenty for our house. I paid for it in anticipation the Land Company will do the right thing with a new contract and hope my instincts are right. I loaded half on the wagon and Thomas promised to bring the other half on his next visit.

First, Ethan and I put sturdy beams over the width of the cottage for a second floor attic room. Next, we winched up the roof supports, built strong to withstand heavy winds.

Rose wants dormer windows but those will have to wait until other necessities are addressed; the outhouse building and barn.

Ethan suggested we frame the dormer spaces into the roof supports though, so when ready, we'll just remove a few slates and build the new dormer windows out.

In one month's time, we've finished the slate roof with everyone's hard work. Even James helped several days a week and has proven himself a strong and steady worker.

Half of the attic floor is finished on the north end of the house over the fireplace and we build a stairway against the front wall near the door. The other half of the attic over the kitchen will have to wait until we're finished outside.

"Oh Daniel, this is so wonderful." Rose exclaims upon getting her first look at the ceiling above. "I can finally get the house clean with no fear of a rainy day. Thank Heaven, you were able to finish before the snows started."

It's enough for me she's pleased. In a few days Ethan will come and we'll get started on the barn.

❧❧

This morning I hear "Rose?" from the front door, and it's Ethan with an armload of something.

"Ethan, you just missed Daniel, he went out back to work on the barn."

"I'm headed out myself." He puts down what looks like towels and sheets on the table.

"These are for you and Daniel. I have way more than I'll ever use and I want you to have them."

"Oh Ethan, these are lovely. Are you sure you kept enough for yourself?"

"Absolutely. Well, I'd best get on out to the barn. See you later."

"Thank-you, Ethan." I call to him and he waves a hand before disappearing out the back door.

The man has shared almost everything he has with us I think to myself. With donations of furniture from his barn loft, we have a bed frame and a new mattress stuffed with feathers Catherine saved over the years.

He insisted we take his old table and chair set, a bowl and pitcher for the washstand and dishes, pans and tableware sets he no longer uses.

I'm most fond of two rockers which will go in front of the fireplace. It's so exciting to finally be moving in and calling this house our home.

❧

Several weeks have passed and my inside work at the farm is temporarily finished. The men travel out every day to work on the barn, but I've been staying back at Ethan's to keep house and gladly cook our meals. His generosity to us is a debt which can never really be paid as far as Daniel and I are concerned.

We'll miss him after the move, he's been both good friend and a brother to both of us, but I have a feeling we'll continue to see him on a regular basis, just not as often.

79

The men are due back soon, a stew simmers on the back of the stove and I've just begun to work on a new rag rug when I hear a quick knock on the front door.

"Who is it?" I ask, rather startled.

"It's Jane."

"Jane? Well for heaven's sake." I unlock the door and she stands forlornly on the porch.

"What are you doing here?" I ask.

She doesn't move, almost as if she hasn't heard me.

"It's Jim," she finally says in a flat voice, "He's gone." Now she begins to sob as James appears from behind her.

"Can we come in Mam? She's been like this since yesterday and I don't know what to do."

"Of course – both of you come in, here let me help you." I put an arm around her waist and lead her to the settee.

She looks thinner than the last time we talked and her eyes are red and swollen.

"What's happened Jane? Did you walk all this way?"

"They found Jim's wrecked boat behind some rocks at the entrance to the harbor. It must have washed up during the storm we had weeks ago and no sign of him or the two men with him."

"Oh Jane, I'm so sorry." She gives in to her grief as I embrace her.

"Can James stay here with you until I find somewhere for us to live? I'm out of money and even with James doing odd jobs I can't afford the rent for our house."

I shudder, remembering Daniel and I were once in a similar situation. If our family hadn't been there for us, where would we be now?

"Of course he can stay and you too." Jane starts to rise from her seat, but I'm quick to say, "You fed us and welcomed us when we arrived and you're both considered friends. At least stay tonight, the men will be back soon from the farm and we'll figure all this out with their help.

"This is Ethan's house so I can't answer for him," I add, "but knowing his generosity, I can't imagine he's capable of putting anyone out on the street."

The men return within the hour and I walk out to give them the bad news about Jim.

Daniel comes in immediately to sit down with Jane while Ethan stands nearby.

"Jane, are you certain it was Jim's boat?" Daniel asks.

"I have no doubt in my mind; his shirt was found wrapped up in the wreckage."

"Rose tells me you've been put out of your house, what about your belongings?"

"Oh Daniel, the landlord wants to keep everything toward this month's rent," She starts to cry again, "our clothes, everything."

"We'll go into town tomorrow and talk to your landlord to see what can be done to get your things back." Daniel says then looks at Ethan who nods and steps forward.

"Daniel and Rose have told me what a good friend you are and how you helped them. You're welcome in my house for as long as it takes to get on your feet."

"Oh Ethan..." Jane starts to say but Ethan interrupts her.

"Now, I won't hear any excuses, you're welcome here and that's that." He turns to Daniel.

"I'm going out to get the horses unhitched."

"I'm right behind you," Daniel answers, "James, you want to help out?"

"Sure." he says and follows them out to the barn.

"I was just putting supper on the table Jane; it's stew and we have plenty. Would you like some?"

"It smells wonderful Rose, if there's enough; yes I guess I'd better make the effort."

After supper, Jane and I sit at the kitchen table with a cup of tea.

"What would you like to do Jane?" I ask. "I mean, where would you rather live; in town or out here somewhere?"

"I'm a townie, Rose; besides it'll be easier to find work in town than out here."

"But what will you do?"

"I can sew, cook and clean but I can't live-in as someone's housekeeper. I want my son with me till he's grown." she says with determination.

"Then it's what we'll concentrate on." I reply. "You have friends in town and I'm sure we'll find something for you." I get up to take our cups to the sink and Ethan comes inside from the barn.

"Let's make a pallet over here by the fire so you can both can get some well-deserved rest tonight." He says. "I'll get some extra blankets."

He hurries off and soon returns with several quilts and blankets, placing most on the floor for a pallet and adding a couple on top with two large pillows.

Ethan steps back and says, "Well, if you'll excuse me everyone, I'm off to bed. Good night." He turns toward his office where he's been staying since Daniel and I arrived.

❧

Later when my house is quiet I lay awake staring at the moonlight through the study's only window. I can't deny Jane's plight has brought back all the old feelings of grief from my Catherine's death and I understand Jane's distress.

I notice something else too; James is trying to be a man about his father's death at twelve years old. Since working with him at Daniel's this summer, I realize what a fine job his mother has done in raising him, but I'd like to see the boy have a chance to be a young lad and free of the heavy load he's carried so early in life.

Somehow, I'll think of a solution to their problems and help in any way possible to get their lives stabilized and happy.

In my heart I feel an attachment to Jane I don't quite understand; but perhaps in the future it will become clear.

❧

This morning Ethan and I take both wagons into town and stop first at the Land Office.

"Good morning Daniel." Mr. MacMillan smiles in surprise as I knock at his doorway.

"Good morning sir; just wondered if you'd heard anything yet from Wellington?"

"Why yes, I received the contract back yesterday, signed and approved.

"They thought your estimate of expenses was very reasonable and I'm authorized to give you this check to repay your own cash already invested in the well and repairs." He says as he picks up a check from a paper weight on the desk then continues.

"I will need to visit during the next few weeks to confirm all repairs; you understand how these things work I trust?"

"I do and wouldn't expect any less. You'll be glad to hear the roof is finished, the well is operable and we've started building a small barn. Our hope is to move in within the next two weeks and give Mr. Shepherd his house back."

"Fine, Daniel, glad to hear it. I'm surprised at the progress you've made in such a short time." He hands me a copy of the contract.

"I couldn't have done it without the help of my friends." I unfold the contract to check the conditions I requested.

"Even James Ferguson who's only a boy carried his weight." I say as I refold the contract which appears in order. "By the way, did you know he and his mother have been evicted from their home?"

"I heard about it yesterday. A terrible situation, I understand Jim was lost at sea. They've lived here many years and I knew Jane's parents up on the North Island before I moved down. Anything I can do?" Mr. MacMillan asks.

"Keep an eye out for a job for Jane; housekeeping, or sewing." I reply then add, "I know she'll do a fine job in whatever she's offered."

"I'll do that Daniel and please, give my best to Rose."

"Will do and I appreciate your working with us on this Mr. MacMillan."

"Please call me Charles and you are certainly welcome."

I return to the wagon to show Rose the check and she breathes a sigh of relief. Our funds have suffered with all the supplies needed for the house repair and this will more than sustain us through the coming year.

"The town bank is open, let's start a new account and deposit the check." I suggest and she agrees.

After the bank, we turn to Jane's dilemma and visit her landlord's house.

Ronan MacDougal opens his door and looks first at Jane then at the rest of us; he seems to recognize Ethan, but moves his glance away quickly.

"What can I do for you folks?" he asks sharply.

Rose and I remember Mayor MacDougal and how pleasantly he greeted us our first day in town.

His mayorship dissolved since a full-time British representative is now assigned to the settlement, he appears rather unhappy and more disheveled than I remember.

"Daniel Smith and Ethan Shepherd;" I say to him, "We'd like to take a few moments to discuss Mrs. Ferguson's belongings. Apparently you've seen fit to claim them for her back rent?"

"I have, but I don't see what it has to do with you sir, now if you'll excuse me."

He starts to close the door but I place my boot directly between the door and its frame to prevent it.

"Mister, if you don't move your foot, I'll make sure you don't use it again, now take it out." He threatens and the tip of his rifle suddenly appears through the opening.

I warn the women to step back but leave my foot in the door.

"Now Mayor MacDougal," I use the old title, hoping to calm the man, "We came in good faith we could work this out and you have no reason to fear us."

"I fear no man and I won't be railroaded into a loss of money over some ragtag bunch of a fisherman's family."

"Then surely you'd be interested in receiving some of your investment back versus a pile of furniture and some clothing?"

The gun tip drops a little then is withdrawn.

"Well, I'd be willing to talk about it." He opens the door to join us on the porch and asks, "What did you have in mind?"

"Jane tells me she's only behind two weeks on the rent; do you agree?"

"Yes that's right, but she can't return to the house even if she pays it. She doesn't have any income now and I won't put up with her kind."

I fight down my impulse to tell him just what I think of his kind.

"Then may I suggest upon receipt of the two weeks monies, you release her belongings so she can be on her way?"

"You intend to pay it?" the Mayor asks as he squints into the morning sun behind me.

Jane starts to step forward to protest, but Rose won't let her.

"That's right Mayor." I use the address again, though he knows it's no longer appropriate and see his demeanor improve at its sound.

"Then as soon as the money is tendered, she can get her things and clear out."

"Very good, Mr. Mayor." I draw out a couple of the notes received at the bank and hold them just out of his reach.

"Now, if you don't mind I'd like a written receipt to state all accounts have been paid up for Mr. and Mrs. Ferguson and her son, with your signature witnessed by Mr. Shepherd and me."

"Give me a moment."

He steps back into the house and soon returns with a receipt form, an ink well and a pen; setting everything down on a small table, he signs the receipt and we witness his signature.

When it's finished, I hand the receipt to Jane and bid Ronan goodbye. We climb back into our wagons to drive to her house and load everything up.

James runs first thing to the little shed behind the house to take care of his goats and is relieved to see they're none the worse for wear after a day without food or water.

We work at packing up the household furniture and fill our wagon and part of Ethan's.

"Any place we need to go while we're all here?" I ask as we finish tying up James's goats behind Ethan's wagon.

James speaks up; "Anyone want fish for supper tonight?" We smile and know things are back to near-normal.

"I think it's a very good idea." Rose says and he quickly walks off with pole in hand to catch enough to feed us all, with plans to meet us later.

"Well, what shall we do in the meantime?" Jane asks.

"Let's go to the Soup Café Daniel and get some lunch." Ethan invites, "I'm buying."

Jane and Rose look at each other first then turn back to him. "Are you sure you want to...go to the Café?"

"Ah-oh, sounds like you may have heard the old rumors." Ethan says with a raised eyebrow.

"Well, we might have..." Rose says uncertainly as she glances sideways at Jane.

"I've known Muriel Taft for a long time," Ethan smiles, "and I'm pretty sure there's no truth to what circulates around this town."

"Well then I say we give it a try." Rose volunteers.

We wind up savoring the soup of the day; a sausage and potato cream soup and order sandwiches to go, with one for James when he meets us later.

It's all delicious and Muriel is a most gracious hostess, especially when she sees Ethan in our group. It's plain she has designs on him he doesn't necessarily share.

"Muriel," Jane asks as the proprietress lingers again at our table, "would you happen to know of any work in town suitable for a woman?"

"What a coincidence," Muriel replies, "I just spoke with Mary Strickland this morning and the seamstress shop is apparently doing well." She looks around the room then leans in closer.

"She needs someone part-time for the hand sewing and finish work."

"Oh how wonderful!" Jane exclaims at the news. "Rose, would you come and introduce me to Mary?"

91

"Of course, let's go." Mary is in the front window arranging new dresses for display when we arrive.

"Rose, how lovely to see you." she exclaims.

"The shop looks wonderful and those dresses are beautiful. Did you design them?" I ask.

"I ordered the patterns from London and they came in last week, so I've been quite busy as you can see."

"Mary, have you met Jane Ferguson?" I ask her.

"Not formally, but I've seen you about town; Jane, very nice to meet you."

"Jane is interested in the part-time position you have open; Muriel Taft mentioned it when we stopped into the Soup Shop."

"I'd love to show you my dress work and let you be the judge Mrs. Strickland," Jane says, "however, I'm between homes right now and most are packed up."

She explains her husband passed recently, but adds "I made the dress I'm wearing."

"Oh my dear, I'm so sorry to hear about your husband. What on earth are you doing for a roof over your head?" Mary asks.

"Rose, Daniel and Ethan Shepherd have generously helped my son and me survive through these hard times and I'm confident we'll be able to settle in a new place soon.

"In the meantime, they've asked us to stay with them. I can be in town every day with no problem or work from home and bring the finished clothing to town on any schedule you decide upon."

"I've seen her work Mary and it's exceptional." I add.

Mary thinks it over for a few moments and makes up her mind.

"Your dress today is quite exemplary; come in tomorrow morning and we'll iron out the details—nine a.m. sharp." she adds with a smile.

"Oh thank-you Mam, you won't regret it." Jane's relief is written on her face and she hugs Mary impulsively before remembering she's her boss then steps back.

"Please, call me Mary. I know I won't regret it and am glad you happened in today. It's a real problem finding someone talented enough and willing to work outside their home."

We say our goodbyes as Daniel, James and Ethan pull up in the wagons.

James has loaded three large fish in an old bucket to the back of the wagon and gulps down his sandwich, telling "fish tales" between bites.

"Shall we stop to say hello to Thomas?" Daniel asks as we near the shop and as we pull up, Thomas waves and motions for Daniel to come in.

"I'm working on your chimney damper and it should be ready to fit by this weekend; will you be out at the farm?"

"We will; stop on by and I'll settle up with you for the job." Daniel answers.

"See you then." Thomas smiles then turns back to his work at the forge.

By the time we arrive home and figure out what to do with all of Jane's things, the sun is setting.

Ethan brings the fish fillets in to me to cook then he and Daniel carry a trunk and one of Jane's beds in from the wagon. We place it on one wall of the living room and hang a curtain around it for privacy.

"You need a good night's rest if you're going into town to work tomorrow." Ethan assures her.

"You're right," Jane answers, "but I'm so sorry for the inconvenience."

"No inconvenience to it, mam." He answers with a slight blush on his face then turns to walk outside and finish unloading the wagon.

The following morning everyone is up as Jane prepares for her walk into town and her first day at work. But when she opens the front door, she finds a buggy all hitched up and ready to go; a surprise from Ethan who cleaned it up for her the night before.

"Ethan, you're doing far too much for me." She says to him.

"Now, don't make more of it than it is; anyone would lend a friend a hand." he says in embarrassment and leaves via the front door to wait by the buggy.

"I am so grateful to you both," Jane turns to Daniel and me.

"Someday I'll pay you back, wait and see. But I have to rush, Mary said 9 a.m. sharp." She quickly leaves after kissing James on his forehead.

Ethan helps her up into the buggy and gives some last minute instructions for the horse after placing a feed bag and water bucket in the back.

"Just tie him up securely at the shop where you can keep an occasional eye on him and he'll be fine."

"I will Ethan."

I watch her drive the buggy out the lane and begin her trip down to the village. She's a good woman I reflect; what a hard life she's had so far. She needs to meet someone when the time is right who'll watch out for her and give her some ease in life. Somewhere inside, I know I could be that man, but it's too soon for both of us right now.

⟨❧⟩

The months since our arrival here have passed quickly I think as I pack up the rest of Daniel's clothing then turn to finish mine.

The trees have shed their lovely gold and red leaves and I'm grateful we'll be moved into our new home before the winter weather begins in June. Already nights and mornings are chill, but the air still warms nicely after the sun comes up.

I look to make sure I haven't forgotten anything then walk to the kitchen for our last breakfast with Ethan who insisted on cooking this morning.

The table is a surprise with plates of bacon, eggs and pancakes, their aroma so wonderful. Jane is here with a day off from the shop and James already lingers at the table to admire its fare.

"Oh my," I exclaim, "I'll be too lazy to move today if I eat all this."

"No you won't, mam." James volunteers with a grin; "I'll help you out and eat your share."

"Very 'helpful' James." I remark skeptically.

After breakfast, we load up the last of our belongings to the wagons, tucking in small items here and there as after-thoughts occur.

Daniel and Ethan took most of the furniture out to the house yesterday so today's loads are mainly supplies; food, grain and smaller items Ethan insists we may need. His generosity continues as usual.

We arrive at our farm and tie the horses out back near the watering trough. The men begin to unload house goods while Jane and I carry in dishes, linens, rugs and smaller items.

I place some dishes on the kitchen table then happen to glance out the back door and notice something unusual just to its right.

When I go out to investigate, Daniel and James stare at me from the wagon; I turn to see what looks like cellar doors against the house.

"Daniel! Oh my goodness!" I can't say more for several moments, as he walks over to me.

"Rose, let me give you the tour" he offers proudly and lays back the big doors from its opening. I take the five steps down into the coolness of a root cellar.

"James and I dug this last week and used rocks off the pasture for its walls. These wooden doors will keep varmints of any kind out." He brags.

"Oh Daniel, it's wonderful." I give him a hug, "What a surprise."

"It'll be shaded all day long back here and in winter I hope to find some ice to put inside which should last us through most of the summer.

"These are shelves for your canning jars and over here, bins for storing potatoes, onions and other vegetables."

"I can't believe you two did this without me finding out." I say with a laugh.

"We were sneaky about it – why do you think I didn't argue when you decided to stay back at Ethan's the last few weeks?"

"So this is what it was all about; I thought you were growing tired of my hanging about." His face goes serious and I regret my pun.

"I will never grow tired of you 'hanging about' my love; you do know it, don't you?" He holds me close now and I notice Jane walk toward us then suddenly turn away.

Over his shoulder, I see her walk to the pasture fence and Ethan follow her. I decide to let him handle whatever is going on with her and pull my attention back to Daniel's embrace.

"I'll always love you Daniel and yes, I know."

Seeing Daniel and Rose together makes me painfully aware of Jim's absence; so much so that I walk away in the opposite direction, stopping at the fence line to take in the view of the pasture land and mountains beyond.

"You okay Jane?" Ethan asks from behind me.

I quickly wipe a tear from my eye, "I envy Daniel and Rose with this new start."

"Yes, it makes me recall past memories, as well." He answers.

"Ethan, how long does it take to stop the hurt after you lose someone?"

"I don't think it ever stops, but time begins to dull the loss and you remember good things instead of just the person's death.

"Look Jane, the important thing for you now is to forge ahead; look for happiness again so you can make a new life for yourself and James."

"Of course you're right Ethan and it's what I intend to do; it's...just hard sometimes."

"It is—no doubt about it. Just know I'll always be nearby if you need a shoulder to rest on. I know we have a few years between us, but don't count me out just yet, okay?"

I can't help but give a little smile at his intimation. "Thank you Ethan."

He turns away to walk back to the wagon and I look after him. He's eight years older, but a handsome, rugged man. We do seem to be kindred spirits...and I feel a bond strengthening between us with each passing day. Lingering by the fence a few more minutes, I concentrate on my son.

I'm aware he hasn't cried yet over the loss of his father, at least not in front of me. He thinks of himself as the man of our house; my fault I know for putting him into the role of breadwinner from early on during Jim's absences.

In a burst of clarity I haven't felt in years, I promise myself to look ahead instead of back and vow as of today to excel at my work and release James from the awful burden he carries.

≈≈≈

"Gidday James." Thomas calls from his forge. I wave to him as I walk to my favorite fishing spot at the dock. It's Saturday morning—no school and I get to fish!

Fewer days to fish has been a problem since I started school in town, but on Saturday, I ride with Mam to the shop and fish all day. The best of my catch comes home and we share with Uncle Daniel and Rose, too.

I sorta miss Mam schooling me at home but after trying the new school for a week, I liked it and haven't regretted my decision to go.

At first we couldn't figure out how I'd get into town to attend, but now I come in mornings with Mam to her work and do my homework in the back of the shop while Mr. Strickland repairs shoes.

Ethan brings me into town on her work-at-home days and I ride back with one of my school chums until either he or Mam picks me up later.

It means I miss working at Daniel's too, but it's a trade I've willingly made. The books at school are a surprise; I can't get enough of them. I'm making good grades and get along with everyone, including my new teacher.

I walk out the dock, empty today except for one small grain ship from the north island that's already unloaded.

It occurs to me the snapper might be eating some of the stray grain that always gets swept from the decks after unloading, so I take out my bit of cotton rag I soaked last night in flour and water for bait.

Sure enough, I feel the tug on my hook and pull in a nice pansize snapper, then another and another until finally I tire of them.

My bait bucket is filled with some mussels off the rocks alongside the wharf and small pilly bait fish; maybe some salmon are about and I rebait my hook.

But just as I get comfortable, a big pelican arrives, landing a few metres from me and I see his two beady eyes focused on my bait bucket.

"I have a close eye on you too, mate." I threaten him.

But between his shiftiness and watching my line, two bait fish are quickly swallowed up and he's alert for more opportunity.

Even after I yell "Shoo" and wave my arms at him, he makes a temporary retreat then returns as soon as my line is back in the water.

I stare at him with what I hope is menace but am distracted by a man and woman talking further up the dock.

"Yes, I believe it's her boy." The woman is looking my way when I turn toward them, but quickly glances away.

"It's just shameful a child is subjected to such behavior."

"I agree and the right thing to do is confide in the Pastor, he'll know what to do." the man concludes.

Not to be outdone, she continues.

"Imagine living out at the Shepherd place without a chaperone and her a widow of not even a year. She obviously has no morals."

They stroll back up the dock and I try to keep my mind on my fishing, but can't as her words repeat in my brain.

What did she mean? She mentioned Ethan's farm, surely she isn't talking about me or my Mam? It doesn't sit right and I take in my line.

At the shop Mam happens to glance out the window and notices me standing in front as I try to figure out how to tell her what I've heard.

"What are you doing out here James? Are you alright?" she asks and descends the stairs to the boardwalk. Instead of looking directly at her, I look away down the street.

"I heard some people talking on the dock. The woman said it's 'shameful' we're living at Ethan's and the man said they should tell the preacher at the church, he'd know what to do. What did they mean Mam?"

My heart nearly breaks because I know exactly what they meant but try not to let James see my concern.

I hug him, "Don't you worry James, people just like to poke their noses into other folks' business, that's all.

"Now go put your fishing stuff in the wagon and we'll head home in about thirty minutes, okay?" I kiss his forehead and walk back inside.

Mary notices what my face must surely be showing and asks, "What's wrong Jane? Anything I can help with?"

I confide in her and for the first time since I've known her, Mary gets angry.

"Oh that woman, I knew she was trouble."

"What do you mean? Do you know who it was?" I ask.

"I have a very good idea it's Muriel Taft. She came in here last week to put a bug in my ear about you at Ethan's without 'suitable oversight' since Daniel and Rose moved to their own farm.

"Oh, I could just wring her neck, may the Lord forgive me, for putting her nose somewhere it doesn't belong.

"I told her right then and there not to be spreading gossip about things she knows nothing about."

"Oh Mary." I sit down heavily on the nearest chair. "What am I to do? We can't afford a place of our own yet, unless it's a tent. We've saved, but we don't have near enough."

"I could speak to George and see if we can bring you on fulltime Jane, but don't get your hopes up, its been rough here for us..."

"Mary, I wouldn't expect it, so please don't even bring it up with George. You've both done so much already.

"I've got to get James home now, but thank-you Mary."

She takes my hand, "Don't you worry Jane, the good Lord always watches over us; you'll find an answer, I know you will."

I walk out the back door of the shop and say goodnight to George on the way.

James already waits in the buggy to drive us home. I climb up to the seat with a heavy heart and he clucks to the mare Jane.

For the first time in the many years I've lived here, I feel conspicuous and alone as we ride up main street. As we pass Muriel's café she pulls the curtains from the window to glance out at me with a smug little smirk. I quickly look back to the road ahead and realize Muriel is my nemesis.

James drops me off at Ethan's front door and takes the buggy on to the barn.

I enter the door and fairly will myself to step inside; I feel as though a fifty pound anvil lays across my shoulders.

Ethan comes out of the kitchen to greet me and notices my expression.

"What is it? James okay?" he asks and moves to look out the back window to the barn.

"He's fine Ethan, it's just...I think we're going to have to move." Tears start to slide down my face and I sit in the nearest chair.

"What do you mean? What's happened? Don't cry Jane, we'll sort it out." He brings a clean dish towel to mop my eyes with.

"Tell me." he coaxes as I gain control.

"James overheard some people on the dock gossiping. It had to do with us in this house under 'improper' conditions."

"Ah, I see. Well, I wondered when those "townies" would run out of talk about their own and start in on us out here.

"Did he know who they were?"

"No, but I confided in Mary and she believes it's Muriel."

"Muriel. So that's it." He gets up to look out the window with an odd expression.

"Ethan, I don't want to create any trouble for you and you don't deserve any. You've been wonderful to us and I'll never forget it but we'll find someplace in town tomorrow. I'm sure something will turn up and we'll move right away."

"No Jane, you don't understand." He says with a deep sigh. "I've never worried about what others think of me. What does bother me is what Muriel is trying to do to you and James.

"Please," his eyes focus on mine, "sit down and let me explain." I sit back down and he takes a seat in front of me.

"Not long after Catharine died, Muriel came out here in her buggy with a dish of food, under the guise of concern for me. I welcomed her into my house and it didn't take her long to try to work herself into my life, if you know what I mean. My wife had just died and the thought of being with someone else, let alone Muriel...detestible.

"I asked her to leave and thought it was all water under the bridge, but apparently our visit to the café last month brought up some old bones to pick.

"That anyone could do such a thing just for spite...is beyond my understanding." He says vehemently.

"I can pay her a visit tomorrow Ethan, straighten her out on what my situation is."

"No, please don't Jane. I think it would just make things worse; she'd turn it around, make it appear you were making excuses."

He lights the oil lamps in the room as the sun takes its last rays over the edge of the mountains behind the harbor then continues to pace a little before he turns back to me.

"Jane, you may not be aware of this, but I'm very fond of you and have been since I first laid eyes on you. I admire your ability to bounce back from the trials you've been through in life and the way you've raised James; good work ethic, Christian upbringing but you're not afraid to let him have a little fun along the way. We seem to share the same ideals and that's good for James...and for us."

I sense where he's headed and try to interrupt.

"Ethan..." But he stops me.

"Now, don't panic Jane, I have to get this out. I've intended to propose to you someday but wanted to give you time to heal from Jim's death and make sure you were ready to be serious again.

"I don't have much to offer to you both except my love and a good secure home. I know it's probably too soon for you to feel anything for me, but I can promise my devotion to you both and I will forever be faithful.

"What do you think?" He almost whispers it and looks scared to death.

"Oh Ethan, it's the most beautiful thing anyone has ever said to me. Forgive me, but I have to talk about Jim a little, just so you understand." I pause to find the right words.

"We married at a young age, pushed by my parents...I already carried James. It's all they could think of to avoid talk in the village and so we married.

"Jim was a good man, but we were very young, only sixteen. I think because he left to fish for long periods of time we were able to stay married.

"We never had the closeness you speak of, but we honored our vows just the same and probably would have continued together, if..."

Ethan takes my hand, "I understand what you're saying Jane and look what a wonderful son you have.

We've all done things in life we wish we could do over differently. I let my wife work herself to death on this farm, all in the name of a dream. We can't change what's already past, only what's to come."

I look into his eyes and see his admiration shining through.

"Marry me Jane, let's start again together. We've learned our lessons, let's make a future for James and for us."

I realise I know him better now than I did Jim when we married. Ethan is a caring, strong and protective man; there's never been anyone in my life like him. I pause only a moment.

"I will Ethan." A giggle escapes; where did that come from I think as I turn shades of pink in embarassment.

"You will? You will!" He picks me up and twirls me around while out of the corner of my eye I see James walk in the back door.

✂∞

They're both laughing together as I enter and I think I know what they may be celebrating but say in a stern voice, "What's going on?" barely able to keep a straight face.

They stop, Ethan puts Mam down and she straightens her hair while she comes toward me.

"James, you know Ethan has been a Godsend to us over the past months don't you? He's provided us shelter and food when we had nowhere else to go?"

I remain silent for effect and she goes on while I struggle to keep from smiling at her.

"I have a great deal of respect for him and he for me, which over time has developed into much more..."

"Are you going to marry him or what?" I say, unable to hold in my smile any longer.

"Yes." They both answer in unison and she grabs me in a hug.

"Oh you're so bad. You knew all along didn't you?"

"Well I may have had an idea." I say and shake Ethan's hand.

He puts Mam and I both in a bear hug for the moment then says, "I'm hungry, let's eat."

We all laugh and sit down to supper to make plans for the wedding next Saturday, here at our house.

Chapter 4 Winter

It's amazing to me as a woman, to see what three men and a half-grown boy can do with a broken-down old farm.

In the weeks since we moved in, Daniel and Ethan have been working on the pole barn out back to shelter the wagon, tack, feed and accumulated tools. Two snug stalls for the mare Jane and a future cow will soon be framed up and we all continue to work on the remainder of the attic floor in the house when it's too cold for barn work outside.

Thomas visits whenever the shop is slow and picks up James to bring along. James, who celebrated his thirteenth birthday last month has developed quite a work ethic and grown about two inches.

He holds his own alongside the men on any chore and fence repair is no exception. It's hard labor setting posts when the earth is cold, but Thomas brought another of his trades from the shop; an auger smaller than the one for the well, with a cross piece for two men to turn. So gradually, the new posts are put in and strung with fence wire from Anderson's.

The remainder of older fencing consists of ponga ferns and a few, laid dog leg style and made from tree branches which will serve well until we can afford better.

Now that we have three large, fenced pastures for sheep and separate roaming room for our milk cow and horse, days fill up with regular farmwork; from the first ray of sunrise to sunset's last spectacular light.

Daniel purchased all the ewe's Ethan wanted to sell and Ethan brought over his ram to turn loose with them for a while. It's winter and Daniel says if it's anything like farming at home, we'll have a good-sized herd started by spring.

I take care of the house and the hen coop where descendants of Catharine's chickens peck their way about our yard.

Two geese are now part of our collection and their loud honks challenge anyone who happens to invade "their" yard. Pecking is not beyond their routine if the person entering is unknown to them and I have more than once rescued hapless visitors from Church who find themselves surrounded in our front yard.

"Rose, why don't you do some canning with some of these birds for the sake of our friends?" Daniel asks.

"I will." I defend myself, "One of them is destined for the table at Christmas, but I want to keep one because I love the way he guards the yard." My husband just laughs and walks away to go on his weekly hunting rounds.

❧

Out in the woods I find five rabbits in my traps. I reset the traps and return to the house to skin and clean the meat. Rose suggests rabbit for tonight's supper and begins scalding glass jars to can the rest for storage in the root cellar.

This afternoon the sun shines through breaks in the overcast sky and a light breeze stirs. The temperature is up a little, enough to allow the remaining snow to melt.

"Going fishing Rose." I call up to her in the loft and hear her answer back from the top of the stairs, "Good luck dear."

I walk through the muddy pasture to the stream and sit on a stump among the cottonwood trees lining the bank. The water flows sparkling, noisy and deep around rocks of assorted sizes and I pull in some nice-sized trout from their hiding spots.

As I move my line there's a glint off something in the water close by. At first, I think it's a fish darting in the sunlight, but now I realise it isn't moving.

Curious, I bend closer to look through the crystal-clear water. By stretching my arm out I can just reach the bottom to grab a handful of pebbles from the mud but dunk my sleeve in the process.

Pulling my hand out of the icy stuff, I deposit its contents on the bank then wring out my sleeve and warm my hand inside my jacket.

When finally I sort through the pebbles and black sand, a partially mud-covered stone shines through. I rinse the mud away to find it's smooth but unevenly shaped. By hefting it in my hand I guess its weight to be maybe two or three ounces.

I try to talk myself out of what my mind is telling me and sit on a nearby stump to reexamine the stone more carefully.

Is it even possible? I know nothing of such things and realise I must talk to someone. I put the stone in my jacket pocket, pick up my fish and head home.

As I walk the pasture I try to put it out of mind; it's just a pretty stone like one from any stream around here I tell myself.

I focus on Ethan and Jane; it's been a while since they've visited. James comes more often with Thomas after school and keeps us up to date on any news. He's doing well in school now; not the same boy who hated reading when we first arrived.

'The teacher is a little stricter than Mum' he said to me with a twinkle in his eye on a recent visit, 'but I make it a point to always be polite when spoken to and stay pretty much in her good graces as long as I do my homework.'

He describes the other students as 'townie pains', but likes having someone his own age to play ball with.

It's good to see him act his age for a change, remembering he was Jane's "little man" for so long. One thing's sure, Ethan has been a good influence on him.

I reach the barn and put the fish in a bucket of water to clean later then wash my hands at the pump.

❧

Ethan and Jane pull their wagon into the front yard just as I finish up some work in the kitchen and I notice they're both smiling when I open the front door to them.

"Hello folks—what brings you out on a Saturday?" I ask them.

"We have some news Mam." James declares from behind them before they can reply.

"Well, come in. It's so good to see you." I shoo them all in.

117

"Good to see you too Rose; is Daniel here?" Ethan asks.

"I think he's back from fishing," and I call him out the back door, "Daniel— Jane and Ethan are here."

I hear Rose from the barn and walk inside to find everyone sitting in front of the fire.

"Hey there." I fake a punch at James playfully as I pass by and shake hands with Ethan. "It's been too long since we saw you folks."

"Well Daniel, you're probably wondering what this is all about." Ethan says, "Plain and simple, I asked Jane to marry me last evening and she's accepted, so we need to plan a wedding."

"Oh my goodness." Rose is out of her seat in a second, hugging Jane and dropping a kiss on Ethan's cheek.

I add my congratulations and give him a hearty thump on the back.

"When does this event happen?" Rose asks.

"We'd like to have the ceremony at Ethan's...our house...next week" Jane answers.

James pipes up, "and you're invited," his voice full of excitement.

"Of course we'll be there. Now what can we do?" Rose asks.

"Good question," Jane says, "nothing is ready; food, a dress and we have to talk to the minister. It will be small, just you folks and we thought to invite Mary and George and maybe Thomas."

"Nothing too difficult I can see." Daniel says, "First things first though, can the pastor make it?"

"We're going to Church in the morning," Ethan adds, "Jane and I."

"Understood. James can stay with us tonight if he'd like?"

"Yes sir; can we go fishing in the stream later?"

"Absolutely. Hear that Rose, I <u>have</u> to go fishing, nothing for it."

The men go outside while Jane and I spend the next hour planning the wedding lunch and discussing what she will wear.

"I still have my wedding dress and I've been thinking; would you like to see it?

"Oh my, Rose...I don't know what to say."

"Then say 'yes' and we'll go have a look." I lead her upstairs and hold up the dress from its place in my trunk.

"This is just beautiful Rose, I'm overcome. I'd love to wear it. It's just what I would have picked for myself;

the high collar, long sleeves and lace over this beautiful satin. And the little veil hat, it's perfect."

While the women stay inside the house making plans, Ethan and I lean against the fence and watch James chase the goose.

We talk about the upcoming planting season and what's new at Anderson's for a while, as I try to think of a way to bring up what's really on my mind.

"I'm having pretty good luck with the rabbit traps. Would you like a couple to take back?" I ask Ethan.

"Generous of you Daniel, sure. A change from fish and lamb would taste good. The ewes will be dropping lambs in a couple of weeks; if you need more, let me know."

"I will but I think if all goes well, I'll have plenty here." I decide to brace myself and bring up the stone from the stream.

"Got something to show you." I say and reach deep into my jacket pocket to pull out the yellow stone.

"What do you think of this?"

Ethan turns it over in his hand and weighs it on his palm. Then he touches it to his mouth and bites down hard on its edge.

"It's almost pure Daniel" he says calmly and waits for me to speak.

"It's...pure? Then you mean...I mean it's..." I sputter and stomp my foot, "It's real."

"Yup, that's what I said, it's a gold nugget." He watches me with a smile then adds, "Some have been found in past years but nothing to get excited over; this might be."

He thumps me on the back several times to start me breathing again and hands the nugget back to me.

"You should keep it quiet Daniel, put it someplace safe, keep it for a nest egg, but don't tell anyone. If you do, you risk having a hoard of people all over your property day and night and more trouble than you want.

"If you don't need the money, keep it for an investment. Anyway, it's what I'd do, it's totally up to you though, of course."

"Sounds like good advice." I say as my mind goes ahead a mile a minute. "It'll take me a while to put this into perspective, I just have to decide what to do now."

The question I don't verbalize; *Are there more?*

∽✬∾

The next morning, Jane and I set out in the buggy to see Pastor Bush. Jane is a little apprehensive since the "gossipers" on the dock were overheard by James to say they would report their concerns to the church, but I try to reassure her.

"If we have to go to the next town to get married, we'll do it. Besides, I've known Pastor Bush for a long time and he has a real talent for keeping "the flock" in check when it comes to gossip.

"Now we're going to services this morning, the same as any other citizens in this town and afterwards we'll talk to the Pastor about marrying us. Are you ready?"

"I am with you by my side Ethan." She drops a kiss on my cheek.

"Well then, let's go." I have a smile on my face a mile wide.

After tying the horse in front of the Church, we step inside just as Pastor Bush takes his place at the pulpit.

We find a seat in the back with Thomas who comes to sit with us and whispers a friendly "Morning."

Muriel sits further down the aisle and one of her friends leans over to whisper something in her ear.

She turns to look back at us and I place my hand over Jane's as she holds her breath for a moment. We both look at Muriel until she turns back around in her seat.

Pastor Bush begins to welcome the congregation to services and asks if anyone has anything they'd like to announce. Muriel stands up.

"Yes, Pastor I do." she says loudly and turns to face the congregation.

"People have come here today who don't belong to this congregation and who blatantly disregard God's wishes with their open and inappropriate behavior. Ethan Shepherd and Jane Ferguson, please leave this house of worship."

She levels her tirade directly at us, even pointing a finger accusingly.

I move from Jane to stand up, but Pastor Bush's voice rises above the congregation members whispering loudly among themselves.

"Please be seated Muriel – Now." The look on his face means business.

Even Muriel sees she may have gone a tad too far and sits down like a petulant child who knows she's overstepped her bounds.

The Pastor comes from behind the pulpit to look over the congregation; some he rode horseback to see in their homes before the Church was built.

"I've known most of you for a long time," he smiles, "shared your worries, your grief, disasters, and death of loved ones." He pauses to look back at me and I nod.

"And thank the Lord, in happy times as well. Sometimes I might have pointed out a scripture to help you through a hard time, or helped you find an answer to a question.

"As a minister of God's Word, I've never been charged with "throwing someone out" and don't recognize it as one of my Christian duties." He looks directly at Muriel, who drops her eyes down and away from his gaze.

"And with that in mind, I'm going to draw some attention to two verses in the Bible which seem appropriate this morning." He returns to the pulpit.

"The first verse is found in John 8:7 and I'm sure all of you know it; Jesus faced a mob eager to execute a woman and He put a stop to it with a simple challenge; *'Let he who is blameless throw the first stone'*. In other words, if you have no sin in your life, step forward and throw the first stone." He pauses to look over the congregation, as if to see if anyone will actually stand.

"The second verse comes from the book of Matthew, Chapter 7, verses 2-5; *'For in the same way you judge others, you will be judged'* What does this mean? It means if we judge with an evil heart or dark intent, His judgment of us will reflect the same." Pastor Bush looks up from the dais to the Congregation.

"Now I've known Ethan Shepherd for a long time and his wife Catharine, may she rest in peace. He's gone through a hard time of it since losing her after fifteen years of marriage.

"I've known Jane for a little less time, but saw her when she came to the Church and asked me to pray for her husband whom she feared was in trouble out on the seas. And indeed, her fears were realised when she lost her husband of twelve years. And as a result, she also lost her home to raise her son in."

This last is spoken with a glance at Ronan MacDougal who squirms in his seat down front.

"How many knew any of this?" A few put up their hands.

"How many offered assistance to our sister, knowing she and her son had been turned out on the street?" None in the congregation hold up their hands.

After furthering the message, the Pastor moves to summation in obvious hope everyone has learned something from this morning's event.

"As we return to our homes to begin another week, let us remember the scriptures today, thanks to our sister Muriel. Do not judge but rather, help one another through life as God commands in his Word.

"We will all need a friend at some time in our lives, and cannot do it alone. If you try, you will fail and harbor regret. And that is the worst burden anyone can carry; it will hold you down by its weight and prevent you from living a full life. Remember, He is our best friend but God inspires and expects us to lend a hand when needed.

"His blessings upon us all, may He relieve us of any regrets we have and wash clean our lives—until we meet again my friends."

The Pastor walks to the back of the Church to see the Congregation off, then returns to greet Jane and me; many come behind him to make us welcome, too.

Muriel glides by quickly with a few acquaintances and leaves the Church behind.

"Thank-you Pastor for what you said today." Jane says.

"Just doing what the good book teaches." He says, "now what can I do for you both today?"

"We've decided to marry and would like you to perform the ceremony Pastor Bush." I announce with a smile.

"Next Saturday if possible, sir." Jane adds.

"I'll be there next Saturday with bells on; I'm so very happy for you both." He answers enthusiastically.

After expressing our thanks and gratitude to the Pastor, we turn our buggy toward the house and talk about our morning all the way home.

"I can't believe Muriel thought she had the right to do such a thing." Jane says.

"She's more riled up than I thought." I laugh, "Wish I could have seen the look on her face when the Pastor credited her with bringing a lesson for the congregation; I'll bet she's seething."

"It could have gone either way and you know it Ethan. We're just lucky that folks are basically good and listen to their pastor."

We ride out to pick up James and when Rose opens the door, a wonderful smell from the kitchen greets us.

"Come in, come in I've got Sunday dinner ready and you're all invited."

"It smells delicious." Ethan says.

A baked chicken, yams and roasted fennel with a sponge cake for dessert are brought to the table and after the food is blessed, Rose can stand it no longer.

"How did it go with Pastor Bush this morning?" she asks.

"He said he'd be happy to come next Saturday and looks forward to it." Jane says and also tells us about Muriel. We are speechless but James stands up.

"The old busy body, she shouldn't get away with stuff like that." Jane grabs his hand and pulls him over to her.

"James, she didn't get away with it; it all came right back at her. Try to understand; God doesn't expect us to judge others around us, just help where we can and conduct our lives accordingly. Words can't hurt us if we don't let them and Muriel will pay in many ways for what she did today, without our hands in it. Understand?"

"I guess so. Just don't take me to eat at her place, because I won't go." He declares and Ethan and I promise him we will not.

ʗɣ

Saturday comes in its usual time and Rose decorated the porch earlier with all kinds of ribbons around its rails to welcome guests.

Pastor Bush, Ethan and I as his best man, stand waiting for Jane and Rose to come to the living room in front of the "window on the world" while George, Mary, and Thomas wait as witnesses.

I pat my vest pocket for the ring Ethan gave me last evening. "Now don't lose this Daniel." He admonished and I tried to appear serious in consideration of his nervousness.

Rose enters then Jane follows in her white wedding dress, her hair in soft curls and the veil about her shoulders from a cap at the back of her head. Ethan's eyes follow her to his side and I can tell he's totally taken with her. They make a handsome couple I think as I look at my Rose and remember our wedding.

Pastor Bush proceeds and at the conclusion, Jane and Ethan kiss as everyone cheers for them.

But James' smile says best what we're all feeling.

Chapter 5   Secrets and Celebrations

Just before dawn I slide out of bed, grab my clothes and leave Rose to get some extra sleep. After putting some coffee on to boil, I sit down to lace up my boots but the chickens suddenly go noisy outside.

I unlock the back door and step outside to investigate but quickly drop back into the shadows. Three men each carry away a chicken from our hen house and don't seem to notice me.

I step back further but tangle with a rake left leaning against the wall. It falls with a loud rattle down the side of the house and the men all turn around.

It's light enough to see these are natives similar to those I witnessed in Ethan's field last year. I decide to step out slowly and wait.

They talk to each other then one comes away from the group toward me. I don't move or show emotion but I sure wish I had my gun.

As he comes nearer, I notice something familiar about him; tall with long black hair, the tattoos and his walking stick, he's the native from the wharf. He continues straight forward and stops silently in front of me. At first he says something unintelligible then he holds out his hand saying "Pleased to meet you."

Startled at the formality of his words, I hold out my hand and say the same to him.

"Pleased to meet you, too." I point to myself, "Daniel."

"Teki" the Maori native says. I hear Rose open the door behind me to see who I'm talking to.

"Oh," she says in surprise. I wish she hadn't come out and I do my best to stand between her and the native.

He looks around me and unexpectedly says "Rose."

She steps forward and offers her hand which he shakes.

"It's the native who traded with me at the docks." she says uncertainly then steps back behind me.

"You're taking our chickens." I point out.

"You on our land...share with us, three chickens twice year and one sheep one in year."

I remember Ethan's words, so I strike the deal and offer my hand on it. The native takes it and looks again at Rose to add, "Woman liked hat."

Rose is a little flustered but says weakly, "Oh, good." He looks back at me.

"You have young?"

"No."

He looks back to Rose, "You wear green stone?" Rose blushes.

"Hmmf." Teki seems to understand and walks back to those waiting for him. They disappear into the thicket that runs along the side of our farm.

"What did he mean about a green stone?" I ask her.

"Come in while I make breakfast and we'll talk." she says with a strange smile.

❧

We sit down to breakfast and before we finish, Daniel asks "Well?"

"It's this," I pull it from my collar and show it to him. "Jane said it's a fertility symbol with the natives."

"I remember it now; you had it at the Church when we were talking with George and Mary. You don't believe in it, do you?"

"Well, this brings me to something else Daniel; remember the feather bed at Ethan's?"

"Of course, what about it?"

"I think you're going to be a father in another five months."

He seems to hear the words but his face goes blank for a moment. Then the full meaning dawns and I can't

133

help but smile. He's out of the chair to pull me into his arms and holds me close.

"Rose, I love you so much."

He's gone from perplexed to happy and I welcome his sudden embrace but just as quickly, he holds me away to search my face.

"Are you alright? Do you need to sit down? I don't want you to do anything more today, I'll do the garden and chickens and housework from here on and don't you worry."

"Daniel—I'm not worried, calm down, I'm fine. I'll do what I feel like and let you know when I need your help, I promise.

"You promise you will?" He repeats and begins to calm down. "We need a bed for him and a guard for the fireplace for when he begins to walk. We'll need..."

"Daniel, you're getting ahead of yourself. Let him...or her be born first. We'll take it step by step, okay?"

"Her. It could be a... little you." He pulls me close again and this time he stays put. I reach to wrap my arms around his neck.

"I love you so Daniel."

"I love you, too."

Later, while Rose is asleep, the night stretches long for me as I lay thinking about my responsibilities to her and my son, or daughter.

We've finished all the repairs to the farm on schedule and several of the ewes are bearing this spring which means we'll have a nice-sized herd to shear and some to butcher in the fall.

I begin thinking about the gold and Ethan's advice. I trust him like a brother; if he thinks secrecy is the better route I'll take his advice. Whatever I find in the stream I'll hide...for a while anyway.

By early morning I decide to choose a secret place inside the house to hide whatever gold I find. Oh yes, I'll be looking for more, no doubt about it, especially in light of Rose's announcement.

I'll tell her about the hiding spot so if something untoward happens, she and our child will be secure in life without me.

The thought jolts me awake again; I want to be here for them both and I vow to take better care of myself. Finally I fall asleep just as the sun starts to peep over the eastern ridge.

Two cups of coffee to clear my cobwebs after a near sleepless night and I return to the stream to take another look. The place I marked on the bank with a fallen limb is isolated from any trails in the area and I sit down to throw a fishing line into the water under the guise of fishing while I try to deal with my discovery.

I'm reminded of old geography lessons in my village school; glaciers over land carved out valleys and plateaus, that much I've retained.

The rest comes slower; precious metals dug deep from the earth and refined by the ice's movement then covered up again by natural erosion.

The stream's wash has widened since the spring rains started and simply uncovered some buried treasure hidden for thousands of years.

I realize, for whatever reason, I've been in the right place at the right time and feel wary now as I look around the field and over to the other side of the stream. A weight lays on me to keep this secret which I never imagined or planned for before moving here.

Yet how can I ignore this and not use it to my family's advantage? It's a gift, a blessing or a curse, its real meaning remains to be discovered.

Kneeling, I again scoop some of the mud mixed with small rocks and dark sand.

My hand is icy but I ignore it this time and let the sand fall slowly through my fingers as I hold my breath.

One nugget then another, both close to the same size as the first lays in my hand. Quickly I stuff them into my jacket pocket and continue to scoop the sandy mud with both hands.

When I return home, my pockets are heavy and I realise I'll need to come up with another way to bring my findings back to the house and a better method to scoop them out as well. My hands are raw and cold from the icy water and I'll rub some lard on them to ease the sting when I return home.

Tomorrow morning right after breakfast, I'll tell Rose.

◈◈◈

"What's wrong Daniel?" she asks with a worried look. I realize my face must be strange as I linger at the table and call her over to sit with me.

"Nothing's wrong, at least I don't think so, in fact everything seems right." I reach into my pocket and draw out one of the large nuggets to lay in front of her. Coincidentally, a sunbeam lays upon it from the kitchen window and the nugget shines.

She picks it up from the tablecloth and turns it over in her hand then looks at me.

"What is it?"

"What does it remind you of?" I ask, playing with her.

"Well, it's a gold color, but surely..." she looks up at me again and sees the smile on my face. "Gold! But where did it come from?"

"Right here on our farm." I answer.

"Oh my word. What do we do next, I mean, we know nothing about such things."

"I took Ethan into confidence, he confirms it's genuine and says some has been found before, but none of any consequence. He advised we keep it secret and hide it for now and I think he's right. We don't need a bunch of miners showing up on our doorstep and walking all over our property."

I pause and think of the other reason which became clear to me last night.

"We don't own this property yet Rose. If the Land Company knew, what do you think they'd do?"

"They'd want to dissolve our contract. Oh Daniel, we can't lose this farm after all the work we've done and I love this place."

"I do too, Rose so here's what I think we must do. We'll make a place inside the house to hide the gold, someplace no one would think to look even if they had suspicions.

"We must never talk about it to anyone, not even Ethan. I trust him as a brother, but gold changes people and I don't want to take the chance, do you ken?"

"Aye Daniel, I think you're right and we must watch how it affects us, too; we can't lose who we are over this."

"I didn't think of that, but you're right. Let's make a pact to remain united when it comes to decisions on this." I hold the nugget up.

"I'd like to continue to put these away for several years; we'll buy the farm per our contract in ten years, but if by then we're tired of this life, we'll have funds to do whatever we want, even a move back to Scotland or maybe to America."

Rose laughs, "Oh you're not changing at all."

I laugh too, "It's nice to have possibilities isn't it?"

"Indeed it is my husband and peace of mind. We've been truly blessed. Just think, if we hadn't taken a chance and left Scotland we'd still be in hardship."

She comes to meet me in an embrace. "It's no wonder I love you so much."

We walk the house to look for possible hiding places and settle upon a loose paver stone in the granite floor by the fireplace.

I remove several pavers and dig a vault underneath then line it with a wooden box 2 feet deep, the width and length of four feet. When the box is filled, I'll simply build another and so on.

I have no idea how to turn the gold into cash, but I'm in no hurry to do so. Plenty of time to figure it out while secrecy is on our side.

✍✍

Winter ends much milder than we'd feared; we were warned temperatures can drop suddenly if storms come in off the southern seas. But we've had only two storms; the last in August whose snow melted by noon with the sun's warmth.

Lambs are on the way already and I'm busy making sure they're healthy and their mothers recovering.

Our milk cow is due to calf soon, fathered by Ethan's bull and we keep her close to the barn rather than wandering the fields.

Even the chickens and geese are sitting as September rolls in.

"Hey Daniel" Ethan calls out as he rounds the corner of the barn this morning followed by James and Thomas. "Got enough work for us?"

I look up in relief, "Enough? You're fooling, right? I've been running on tired for days now, the ewe's all

140

seem to be delivering around the same time." I stand up to greet my friends and James comes to see the lamb just born.

"We have lambs too, how many do you have?" he asks.

"Fifteen so far and more to come. You didn't tell me your ram was a mover Ethan." I shake his hand then Thomas's.

"Don't look at me, I'm a blacksmith, but if you need help with shearing later, I'm pretty good. Besides I have a new design for shears I'd like to try out."

"You're hired. Come on up to the house and we'll have a cup, I need a break. James can you keep an eye on this one for me?"

"Yessir." The thirteen year old says and straightens his shoulders with the responsibility. Ethan admires his new son, who's growing into a fine young man.

Rose has a pot already brewed; cups and some shortbread are on the table.

"How're you feeling Rose?" Ethan asks since we've told him the good news.

"Oh, I'm fine Ethan." she says, blushing.

"You've been sick Rose?" Thomas asks with concern.

"She's expecting in a few months Thomas." I say as I glance at her.

"Well congratulations to both of you, what good news."

"Yes, Daniel has practically made an invalid of me and won't let me help him much around the farm, but I know he means well." Rose responds with a smile.

Ethan speaks up first, "Then we need to see what we can do to share a little of the load Daniel and don't argue with me.

"James is coming along as a crack rancher, taught him quite a bit around my place with the sheep, cows, chickens and the like. If you don't mind his age, he could be a real helper for you, at least through birthing time this spring."

"I might be ready to take him on, if it won't put too much on you Ethan or his school work?"

"I sold off enough stock last summer, so I can handle what's left by myself. You're welcome to ask him, see what he says."

James accepts with a resounding "Yes." to my relief. He'll finish the school year working afternoons then decide if he wants to continue to high school or work fulltime.

In January, Rose goes into labor during the night and in the morning, I send James home to get his mother and bring her back while Ethan goes on to town to fetch the midwife.

When Jane reaches the farm, I'm pacing nervously and open the door before she has a chance to lift the latch.

"I'm so glad you're here Jane. She started sometime last night and woke up this morning in pain."

"She'll be alright Daniel, let me go up to see her alone then you can come when I call you." I watch as she climbs the stairs to the loft where Rose lies on our bed.

"Jane I'm so glad to see you, I didn't expect this to happen so soon." Rose smiles but I can tell the pain is taking a toll on her.

"How close are the contractions?" I ask.

"I think about thirty minutes."

"You've got a way to go but you'll be just fine. Ethan went to town to fetch the midwife and she'll be here soon."

"Thank-you Jane, you're such a good friend." Another wave of contractions starts and I hold her hand.

"Just remember to breath." I coach; remembering James's birth, I watch her labor through the pain.

When the contraction subsides, I return downstairs to ask Daniel for some supplies and to put on some hot water. I don't really know if the midwife will make it, but won't tell Rose or Daniel just yet.

Two hours later it's become evident Daniel and I will be delivering this baby.

"Daniel," I call downstairs, "will you come up please." I hear his feet on the stairs, two at a time.

"Is she alright?" he asks anxiously.

"Yes, she's doing fine and in fact it's time to start bringing this baby into the world." I concentrate on keeping my voice light so he'll remain calm.

"Now Daniel, you'll be receiving the baby while I cut the umbilical cord, since it doesn't look like the midwife will make it."

I've already noticed a temporary bed for the baby made in a dresser drawer and plenty of baby blankets and swaddling are ready nearby.

Daniel is a little shaken, but he seems up to the task. He crosses to Rose and kisses her forehead.

"Are you ready for this?" he asks softly.

"Yes, of course love, I can't wait to see our little one."

"I love you my wife." He steps aside to let me take over.

"Alright my sister," I concentrate on Rose, "the baby has crowned and it's time. When your contractions start again, you're going to push."

"I'm ready Jane" she says and it doesn't take her long to deliver a fine baby girl, with soft blonde hair and pale skin.

I clear the baby's mouth and cut the cord then close up the blanket Daniel received her in. She cries a little, but quiets and sleeps as he cuddles her against his chest. Rose is overjoyed and can't wait to hold her.

"Oh Jane, more pain is coming." She looks to me in distress.

"The after-birth will expell; let me take a look." Upon examination I smile and say, "Rose, are you ready to go again? You have another baby on the way!"

In about ten minutes I wrap another fine daughter in swaddling and tuck her into Daniel's other arm.

"Here you go Daniel, one for each arm."

"Oh my..." he says in astonishment. This little bairn has dark hair and long lashes.

My heart is overflowing as Jane gives me my second daughter; whether to laugh or cry, I do a little of both as any father would.

After making sure my beautiful wife is recovering well, Jane steps away so Rose and I can have the moment. I place our babies, one in each of Rose's arms, then lay down with my arm across them all. Jane is downstairs updating Ethan and the midwife who have just arrived.

"I have everything I ever wanted right here." Rose says as I play with one of our daughter's hands.

"I feel the same way my love. Two beautiful babies at once; it's truly amazing."

"Do twins run in your family?" she asks.

"Never heard of any."

"None in ours either. It's just a blessing God thought to give us." She beams at me.

The midwife comes upstairs to check her over and announces all is well and the babies are perfect.

Ethan and James come next to see the new arrivals, giving their approval of the wee ones.

❧❧

A baptism is set for February 28, 1849, a fine late summer day it is, when we each hold a wee one for Pastor Bush to ask the Lord's blessings upon.

We decide to name them after their grandmothers; Kenna, my mother's name for our dark-haired beauty and Briana for our little blonde gal, after Rose's mother.

Jane sewed beautiful white dresses for both babies, with pink roses embroidered along the hems and ribbon bows down the fronts with little caps to match.

Those in the Church today have fallen in love with them, even when they wake to fuss as the water is pressed upon their heads.

⧉⧉

Our year of new parenthood has sped by and we are once again blessed in this October to welcome a bonny son born with the midwife in attendance, though Jane came along for moral support.

He comes with no twin to follow but makes up for it with a strong voice and weighs considerably more than each of the girls did. I hold the wee laddie and marvel at his full head of dark hair and fists which are quite strong when wrapped around my finger.

The midwife speaks to us both before leaving and warns Rose should abstain from becoming pregnant again for at least a year and give herself time to mend. There's a tear she sustained during the birth; the closeness to her last pregnancy and her long labor taxed her strength significantly this time. We agree our family has come along well and a break is needed, if the good Lord wills.

Both Briana and Kenna are walking and very curious about the new arrival. They kiss his forehead and always come when he cries.

Though too young to do much but stand by his crib until one of us arrives, it is beautiful to see them so concerned on their brother's behalf and to hear their coos and baby-speak to him.

When it comes time for the christening by Pastor Bush, we decide to name him Angus after my father in Scotland. It's a fine strong name and we pray he'll be blessed to live up to it with pride, wisdom and humility.

Chapter 6 Choosing Sides

This New Year's day of 1860 I stop to gaze out the barn door at my sheep in the fields. It's three years today I made good on the contract to buy the farm and closed the deal through an agent of the British government in 1857. The Land Company, long out of business by then, turned over their remaining contracts to the government to resolve.

I think of my Rose and wish she could have seen the day with me before she was taken. It's a thought which brings pain, even more intense when I remember the unborn son who went with her. I stand too often recounting those days and it seems nothing I do can be right without her.

I finish putting up feed for the horse and chickens in the barn and lock the door securely to keep scavengers out of it, rodent or otherwise, then pick up the lantern for the walk to the house.

The kitchen window is bright with light and cheers me, especially when my daughters pass by it as they prepare the evening meal. Angus will be home soon from Ethan's where he's been helping James with barn repairs. Thank God for the children.

My spirits lift the moment I open the back door and set my boots on the mat which Kenna insists I use to keep her floors clean.

"Dad, can you go back out and pull a few carrots to have with dinner?" Briana's blue eyes sparkle as she makes the request; what father could refuse those eyes, thirteen and already so beautiful.

Willingly, I push the boots back on and walk to the kitchen garden, still in the same place Rose started it those first few months. I quickly pull a dozen carrots, rinse them under the old pump and toss them into a bucket.

Briana waits in the kitchen, "Thanks Dad" she smiles and plants a kiss on my cheek.

"Welcome my daughter." I hold her cheek for a moment before going to the washstand to splash some water on my face and get ready for dinner. Angus comes noisily through the front door with James following behind.

"Look who tagged along for dinner." He announces as he hangs his jacket on a hook and heads to the basin.

"James." Both girls exclaim and go to give him a hug.

"Why is it we hardly ever see our Uncle James anymore?" Kenna asks.

James blushes and jokingly replies, "Unlike Angus here, I'm working long hours and going to school."

He receives a boxing from Angus and laughter from the girls then comes to shake my hand; "Good to see you Uncle Dan."

"And you." I exclaim. "How's your Mother and Ethan?"

"They're fine. Michael keeps them busy chasing him all over the farm, but other than that, they're good."

Ethan's son was born a year after he and Jane married; a gift he'd said, since he had no hope of ever having a son at his age. They named him after Jane's father and Michael's grown tall and strong like his Dad, twelve years old now; and James is twenty-six.

"Well, come sit down everyone, its ready" Kenna calls from the kitchen and we gather to feast on the girls' cooking, both of whom are so good at it. "Lamb stew tonite, from mother's recipe." Brianna adds.

"What are you planning for the new year Uncle Dan? Acquiring any new animals?" James asks.

I think on his question for a moment; "Nope, no plans yet but something will turn up."

Each year I seem to acquire a new tenant for this farm though never planned. The year before last I bought a new horse to replace the mare Jane who stepped in a hole and broke her front leg. I had to put her down but it couldn't be avoided.

Thomas helped me find a new mare, a chestnut brought down from Wellington by a resident who decided to sell out and move back north again. She has a white blaze and Kenna and Briana named her Sister. They continue to spoil her with the best feed and care and she's a beautiful sight pulling the buggy.

Last year I happened to be in Anderson's for some supplies and heard a noise behind me. When I turned around, there in a cage on the dusty floor, was a white terrier pup who couldn't have been more than ten weeks old. His mother came from England and died during transport on the ship shortly after his birth.

I tried, Lord knows I tried, but I couldn't walk away. Thinking of the girls, I paid for him and put the pup inside my jacket for the ride home.

When I walked into the house, the pup started whining from his warm hiding place and I stood nonchalantly as both Kenna and Briana asked about the sound. I denied hearing it, they laughed and came over to open up my coat. With many oohs and ah's, they made the pup comfortable with food, water, a blanket bed and much cuddling.

Per the girls his name had to be 'Jim', after James, the reason never clear, but it does seem to fit.

❧❧

Angus grabs more bread then says, "James, I hear the natives were in the village and stole some chickens from behind the soup kitchen."

"Oh? Where did you hear? Were they caught?" I ask and notice Daniel slowly puts down his spoon and picks up his tea for a long draught.

"It's going around school." Angus replies rather nonchalantly, "They weren't caught but Muriel Taft is fit to be tied. Says she's reporting it to the Superintendant on Monday."

After wiping his mouth, Daniel looks at Angus and then to me before returning to his meal.

"Dad, why do we give our stock to the natives; what kind of hold do they have over us?" Angus asks.

I've known for years Daniel shares a common bond with my stepfather Ethan. They've been "paying" part of their stock to the local Maori leader known as Teki Haku for years, but I also know firsthand of Muriel Taft and her affinity for making everyone's business hers.

153

I look back at Angus who confided to me recently he doesn't understand why Daniel continues to share with the Maori, now that he owns the farm. But I can't believe he's picked this time to bring it all up.

Daniel finishes his last bite and pushes his plate away.

"They have no hold over us son. There aren't enough of them left to do that after settlers and fortune-seekers beat them down over the years, infected them with disease, took their land away with lies and false promises. They have their pride, but it's hard to feed your babies with pride." He rises from his chair, still looking at Angus.

"It's a small thing to share what we have with a few peaceful natives left over from another era."

He goes to get his jacket, "They don't deserve to have the authorities called on them and for their sakes, I hope Muriel comes to her senses before she starts more than she can finish. I'm going out to check on the animals."

After Daniel leaves, Angus and I continue to talk quietly about it then settle down to play a game of cards. I decide to stay on the couch tonight but promise myself I'll talk to Ethan when I go home tomorrow.

When Daniel returns to the house, the girls and Angus have retired to their rooms and I'm camped out on the couch. He tells me he's decided to accompany me home in the morning and have a talk with Ethan.

It's late at night and I still lay awake thinking about Angus and his remarks. I realise no one is to blame but myself as a father for failing to talk to him about the natives.

I saw Teki three months ago when he came by to collect his annual ewe and we talked a little about wives and children. During the years we've built a trusting relationship and since Rose's death, Teki always asks if I've remarried and how the children are.

He's become thinner and his age is showing. He brings younger members of his whanau, his family, with him to carry the ewe away. It's easy to remember him on the wharf our first day and hard to see him so changed.

With true native honesty, he talks of when he will sail the sky someday soon. I wished him well as he left and he spoke in the British school phrasing he'd been taught as a young man; "Good day to you sir."

155

I finally close my eyes but promise myself I will seek an opportunity to talk with Angus soon, so that he understands.

⊷⊶

"I'll just get saddled up too, James." I say this morning as he prepares to go to the barn for his horse.

"Can I come too Dad?" Angus asks and I nod to him.

"Any company appreciated." James says.

When we arrive at Ethan and Jane's, a strange rig is parked in front of the house. Angus walks our horses back to the barn while James and I go inside.

Ethan sits at the kitchen table talking with the village Superintendant and we excuse ourselves for interrupting.

"It's no problem, come in." Ethan says almost with relief and stands up to introduce us.

"Superintendant Anderson, this is Daniel Smith who lives down the road and this is my son James." Anderson shakes hands with us both, seeming to concentrate on me with a little too much interest.

"Please sit down Daniel" Ethan says, "You want some coffee, I just made some fresh?"

"Sure, sounds good" I pull out a chair but James retreats back to the barn.

"Mr Smith, I understand you may know the local Maori tribesmen in some way, is it true?"

"You don't hesitate to ask the interesting questions do you Mr Anderson?" I smile. "This have anything to do with the theft I heard about yesterday?"

"Yes, actually I'm trying to find out the facts behind a complaint I received and would appreciate hearing your answer."

"I've seen them off and on over the years." I take the hot cup of coffee Ethan hands me.

"Have you ever had trouble with them taking things from your property?"

"No, no trouble." I answer calmly, looking directly at him.

The Superintendant writes something into a notebook he has open on the table and I take another sip.

"I've received information you and some of the other ranchers have been forced to give a portion of their livestock to these natives as protection against theft, is this true?"

"I've never given any of my livestock to natives, or to anyone else under force Mr. Anderson. I have however, given to several different families in the area

157

with a clear need and when I can make a difference in their lives by a donation."

"And were some of those donations to natives Mr. Smith?"

"I prefer the identities of the recipients remain anonymous Mr. Anderson, I'm sure you can understand."

He continues to write in his notebook and doesn't look up when I refuse to name recipients. I decide this is a good time to take my leave.

"Ethan, thanks for the coffee, its getting late and I'm expected at home. Superintendant, good to see you again, if I can be of further assistance in this matter, please let me know." I cast my eyes to Angus who entered during the conversation; "You ready?"

When we're down the road a way, I choose the moment to open up a little with Angus.

"You know you can't talk about what goes on out here to any of your school friends, right?"

Angus squirms in the saddle; "I might have hinted at some contact with natives out here in the country, but what if I did? It isn't a crime to talk about them is it?"

"It's no crime son, but do you see where it can lead? Ethan and I become targets for interrogation, just by the fact we see natives out here. So whenever anything occurs in town and anyone even thinks it might be natives, here comes the Superintendant, doing his job to get to the bottom of it via us."

"I'm sorry Dad, but what right does he have to question us? We live out here on our own property and it's a town matter."

I pull up my horse by the stream and Angus does the same. "We need to have a talk son."

"Am I in trouble?"

"No, you're not. I blame myself for not having this talk with you before today, but now I want you to know somewhat of what you speak so bravely."

We both sit down and lean against a cottonwood tree.

"I want you to begin understanding the country we live in and its people. The natives, the Maori, were here hundreds of years before they even knew white men existed. Their history is way older than ours and they believe their people were once gods. This land we all think is ours, was given to them by their gods to live on and command forever."

"Well it's just wrong Dad. You bought our farm and you and Mother worked hard to develop it."

"But Angus, do you ken how our work looks to the Maori? If you believed in something handed down over generations and some pakeha came from the sea and told you differently, would you just accept it?"

"No, I guess not."

"Your Mother and I were poor in Scotland as were many then. We left everything and everyone we loved to come to New Zealand because we were told 'rich farmland is available at good prices'." I look at him before continuing.

"We weren't told land was being taken forcibly from its original owners or the treaty made between the natives and representatives of the Crown could not possibly be supported and its promises broken. And we weren't told of the continuing land wars on the North Island between the tribes. We found out about all this after we arrived."

I hang my head for a few moments then take a drink from the stream. Splashing my face, I dry off on my sleeve.

"I feel sick inside whenever the natives visit us and I think of the conditions under which they must raise their children. I don't give them a share of my stock out of fear, I give it willingly to assuage the guilt I feel as a pakeha on their land." I stop in front of him.

"Do you think the Superintendant would understand or even care about it if I told him the truth?"

Angus looks up at me in understanding, "No, he probably wouldn't Dad."

"One more thing you need to realize; Superintendant Anderson has every right to question anyone within his jurisdiction. He's charged by the Queen to keep the peace and uphold the Crown's government."

I offer him a hand up and Angus takes it, standing almost as tall as me now, I hug him roughly.

"Anytime you want to talk about this, come to me. I'll answer any questions I can, okay?"

"Ok." Angus smiles as he climbs up on his horse and rides with me towards home.

❧

It only took a week to receive papers requesting I appear before the Superintendant for further questioning. I ride to town this morning, stopping off to see Ethan on the way.

"Morning Ethan, looks like rain today." I say as he opens the door to my knock.

"You come all this way to discuss weather Dan?" he asks with a half smile.

"I'm on my way to meet the Superintendant and thought you might have some words of advice."

Ethan hasn't received anything himself, but knows it's just a matter of time.

"Wish I could say I did Dan, but these things have a way of working out no matter what we do. Want some coffee?"

"Sure and any coaching you can give me would be appreciated, too."

He joins me at the table with the coffee. "Answer his questions simply, don't add anything not in the original question. If you don't feel the question deserves an answer, say you don't know. Don't be concerned it may make you look like a fool, we both know you're not."

"Thanks mate." I drain my coffee cup before heading for the door.

"Stop by on the way back and let me know how it goes. Get word to me if the odd thing happens and you need help, do you ken?"

"Aye." I say with little enthusiasm.

I arrive early enough to sit in the waiting room and watch some of the activity in the office which seems unusually busy.

The local constable comes through asking the secretary to see Mr Anderson, then enters and closes the door heavily behind him.

I hear voices raise behind the door before all goes quiet. When he leaves, he notices me and touches his hat.

Anderson comes out to motion me in. I sit quietly in front of his desk and wait for him to take the initiative. He brings out what looks like the same leather-bound notebook used at Ethan's last week and silently reads his notes.

"You've been here how many years now Daniel?"

"We, my wife Rose and I arrived in the fall of 1847."

"My, you've seen some growth and change. Have you and your family been happy here?"

"I lost my wife and a third child with her five years ago. Life has been different since, but I treasure our farm and my children."

"I'm sorry Mr. Smith, I didn't know about your wife, I am truly sorry. How long have you known Ethan Shepherd?"

"Since the second day we arrived." I remember what Ethan said and wait for his next question.

"That's quite a while, do you consider him a friend?"

"Yes."

"What can you tell me about his dealings with the Maori?"

"I am unaware of it Mr Anderson."

"Still giving donations to the needy Daniel?"

"It hasn't come up lately but yes, if the need arises I consider a well-placed gift appropriate." I look straight at him as I say it.

He gets up from his chair to walk around his desk and lean on its corner.

"I thought you and Ethan would like to know the Constable caught the thieves reported last week, a couple of young men recently off a cargo ship from Auckland." He walks to take a look out the window before turning back to me.

"They were a little short of cash and hungry, so they decided to help themselves to some 'free' chickens behind Muriel Taft's shop. They took them outside town and proceeded to roast them on an open fire. The smell wafted over to a nearby neighbor who discovered them and called the Constable.

"The reason I've summoned you is because Mrs. Taft made some extraordinary accusations along with her report of theft, concerning how you and Ethan conduct your day to day affairs, specifically with regard to the few Maori in this area. Because she included this information, it became my responsibility to investigate via my appointment and report back to the Crown."

"I can't believe the Queen is interested in two small town farmers like myself and Mr. Shepherd. What's the real story here sir?"

"You're wrong Daniel, believe it or not, land wars still seeth under the surface on North Island. Lives have been lost and the problem remains.

"We, on the other hand enjoy a modicum of peace here and wish to see it continue. The Crown is aware not all settlers seek to fight and want only to live on their land in peace, raise their families and grow old in comfort. Some people have found a way to do that with all their 'neighbors', shall we say?"

I look at him in mild surprise; is he saying what I think he is?

"At some point, the Crown may have need for men who are acquainted with the local natives here on South Island, so it has become part of my job to identify these men.

"I've been directed to invite them to assist the Crown, be available should difficulties arise and enlist them in a hometown militia."

"I'm not a politician or soldier Mr. Anderson, I'm a farmer and have no interest in matters of State."

"But you would, I assume, heed the call to help as much as possible should a 'mediation' be needed between natives and settlers?"

I roll his suggestion around in my head; "I'd be available if you think I could be useful, yes."

"Very good Mr. Smith, your Government is grateful. Of course we hope none of the business going on in the North comes our way, but it never hurts to be prepared does it."

He reaches into his desk and pushes a paper toward me.

"Please read and sign this so I can put it in the file for any future reference, as we discussed. No training will be involved as you'll be unarmed, unlike regular militia."

When I finish the paper, he escorts me to the door.

"What about the accusations of Mrs. Taft?" I ask, "Will your findings be posted in the news so the real story is revealed?"

"Yes, the Constable routinely releases all arrests to the local paper and I'll personally be speaking with Mrs. Taft later today to let her know the true culprits in the theft. I'll also be cautioning her on any future accusations in such a public manner.

"Her allegations could be construed as slander if pursued legally by the innocent party, resulting in a rather large settlement against her. Good day Sir." I detect a slight upward curl at the corner of his mouth.

"Thank-you Superintendant and a good day to you, too." I certainly feel much lighter of foot than when I entered his office.

168

Chapter 7   1861-1866

'Gold Found in Otago Province' the headlines declared. Excitement continued to churn through the town citizenry long after they read their June 1861 weekly newspaper.

The town of Lawrence and a man named Gabriel became famous after he shovelled through some gravel in a creek bed one day.

Sounds rather familiar I thought as I read the site was named after him later as 'Gabriel's Gulley'. Maybe they'll name the stream after me, but then I reminded myself someone would need to know about my find and I wasn't ready for that yet.

With the news going public, local shopkeepers, officials and even farmers-turned-miners equipped at Anderson's Warehouse to make the trip to Lawrence and the gold fields beyond. Older settlers in town told me gold has always been here but never in an amount to raise a miner's blood pressure until the Gulley. Miners from other countries began to flood into our seaports.

Prosperity came to all, especially the provisioners, the shipping industry and the banks. Gold fever was upon the people and I didn't like what I saw as local governments scrapped with their neighbors over their "share" of gold revenues and taxes.

The Maori's apparently knew the yellow-colored stones well but valued their green stones for trading, purchasing and showing status. Soon though, even they succumbed to mining for themselves after finding pakehas searching for gold on their land.

Since then I continue to keep my own discovery secret and watch the news where I've learned more on how gold is found, mined and sold to banks and their agents.

I've also become painfully aware of the danger involved; rising crime, robberies of bank reps in the field, claim jumpers, theft of goods and supplies from provisioners and sometimes, murder. Mounted gold escorts hired to bring gold from the fields to the banks, now also serve to bring down 'prisoners' from the fields to the local constabulary for holding until dispositioned by a circuit court judge.

By 1865 the "fever" on our eastern coast subsided with most of the Otago claims worked out. New discoveries were made on the western and northern shores of New Zealand and our town, grown fat with the rush, settled down again as miners and the money they generated traveled away to the west.

On the North Island, unrest among Maori and the British has heated up with the death of a German-born missionary at a mission station in Ōpōtiki. Hung by his own native congregation out of distrust, he was beheaded, his eyes plucked out and eaten by the tribal leader. I am appalled as I read it and wonder where the killing will lead.

During the past year, I've increasingly felt the time is right for me to move forward with plans for our gold and this summer evening I sit at the kitchen table to begin a plan.

The house is unusually quiet since Angus and his sisters are at Ethan's to help with one of Jane's projects.

I look around at this home Rose and I built and remember evenings when chores were done. She'd come down the stairs to the kitchen in her robe and look so beautiful; staying up without complaint during lambing season to make me coffee through the night.

Many a time our children played on the rug in front of the hearth, while she and I sat together watching them. Now, only the clock in the kitchen tick-tocks and the silence is heavy.

Since her death, my enthusiasm for life has been missing. I've tried to deny it for the children's sakes, but without Rose, the years ahead look empty to me. It's time to count my assets and try to figure out the future.

I think I know roughly how much gold lays beneath our floor after weighing each load on our feed scale in the barn. But considering the latest total, it's clear I can't do this by myself.

My thoughts turn to Ethan, my good friend over the years. I trust him to help with the gold's transport and to assist in determining the best way to manage it. The sheer size of the endeavor sets my head to spinning and I stop for the night. *Rose should be here* I think as sleep gradually overtakes me.

This morning I awake to the geese honking in the yard and when I look out the dormer, Ethan is tying off his horse at the back door.

I call down to him through the window. "Hey, you're around early"

"Got any coffee?" he asks.

"Be right down."

At the back door, he pulls off his boots to leave them on Kenna's rug.

"Sleeping in this morning?" he jokes, noting my uncombed hair.

"Late night; have a seat, I'll put the pot on. To what do I owe this visit?"

"Nothing special, Jane has a bunch of women in for the morning, sewing for some wedding in town – your daughters are over helping her, remember?" I nod and put two cups on the table.

"Angus and James are fishing in town and I don't expect them back until all the women leave."

I pour the coffee and put out some biscuits and jam the girls made before leaving yesterday.

"As it turns out, I'm glad you happened by. I need your expertise and common sense; mine is spent at the moment."

"Okay, I'm available – what's going on?"

"Remember ten or so years ago I showed you the nugget I found?"

"Hard to forget,.." He takes a swallow of his coffee and reaches for a biscuit, "you've never talked about it so I figured you didn't find anymore."

"Well, not exactly..." I try to think of a subtle way to tell him about it but realise there is none.

"I've gathered approximately 5200 pounds of ore over the last ten years." My timing may be a little off as Ethan tries to swallow his coffee.

He begins to cough and I jump up to thump him on the back until he recovers.

"You really know how to aid a person's digestion. Did you say 5200 pounds?" He asks, his face still red.

"Aye. I think the time to examine my options is here and you're the only one I trust enough to talk about it with. Three things occurred to me last night; the first, to weigh with more accuracy than on my feed scales, so I have a handle on the quantity."

"Good point; let me mention Thomas has a regularly calibrated scale he uses for iron, but it would involve bringing him into your confidence; it's up to you."

"It's a good suggestion." I say as I get up to clear my mind and stretch. My eyes fall on Briana's drawing of Rose and I walk closer to stare at it.

"Years ago Rose and I talked about what gold does to people and we decided not to tell anyone and keep our friendships simple. I've never regretted our decision, nor have I any reason to doubt either you or Thomas."

"Appreciate it Daniel" Ethan answers.

"If the gold value is sufficient, I'm considering selling the farm and returning to Scotland. I have to clear it with Angus and the girls first; if they want to stay, I'll give the farm to them to run."

"Hold on here – you're getting off the track of gold and already moving back to Scotland. I understand its your homeland Dan, but things have changed since you knew it. Are you sure?"

"I'm not sure of anything yet, except I've been given the chance to change our family's long history of working class dependence to independence. I'd like to put my knowledge of the granite industry to work and partner a granite business in Aberdeen. From all news I read, granite has recovered, flourishing even and I'd like to return."

"Jane and I've known you well for years Daniel, I don't like to think of your moving away but, if it were me I might do the same."

"Lastly, when I do cash the gold in, word will be out and the mining insanity will begin on our back door step. I hate doing this to you and Jane. We've been lucky for the most part in having peace and quiet out here but it may be over."

"I don't expect you to do anything but what works for you and your family." Ethan replies. "A man can't stop progress, be it what he wants or otherwise. If you weren't here, someone else wouldn't have handled it half as quietly."

"One other option occurs to me; if we decide to leave, are you interested in the farm, or in mining any gold left?" Ethan sits back in his chair with surprise.

"Interesting idea Dan, you're full of them today aren't you." He remains quiet while I finish off my coffee then says, "I think we can talk about it later. If I consider it, it would be on one condition; we split fifty-fifty on profit from further discoveries."

"I don't know a lot about gold Ethan, except picking it up over the past ten years; excavating it or bringing in equipment to extract it is another matter and the cost needs to be part of our decision. We can consider putting it out for bid and have better control of the situation...what do you think?"

"I think all these ideas are good ones and we can cross those bridges as we come to them. Right now the weighing of the lot and bringing your family into it are your two top priorities, as I see it. If you want, we can go into town and visit with Thomas later, when you're ready."

"Agreed; the second one is scary. I don't know how Angus and the girls will see this and guess I'd better get to it, the sooner the better." As if on cue, we hear the buggy pull up out back.

Angus jumps down to help the girls out and ties Sister to a post until he can brush her down and feed her. When they enter the house they see us sitting at the table with, I imagine, rather strange looks on our faces.

"Everything alright?" Angus asks.

Ethan and I both answer at the same time, offering a mixture of blended phrases such as 'fine', 'good morning' and 'sure thing'.

Angus looks at Kenna and she looks at Briana, who heads over to plant a kiss on my cheek. "Did you miss us?"

"Sure did." I say, "But the biscuits made up for it."

"Okay Dad, what's going on?" Kenna asks as she comes to sit down with us. I look at Ethan and back at my family, who by this time are all peering at me expectantly.

"Well, I'm just going to get on home Daniel." The coward gets up from his chair, "Thanks for the coffee and biscuits. You want to take care of the business we discussed, tomorrow?"

"Sounds good, I'll be at your house in the morning." I walk him to the door, "Appreciate it."

"Don't mention it."

I turn around to see all eyes still upon me.

"Alright everyone, we need to have a family talk and it might take a while. Angus, go take care of Sister, when you're ready we'll sit down and get started."

When all are seated and Angus brings the cookie jar to the table, I quiet their questions saying, "We've been blessed with an unexpected windfall. Everything we talk about today is to remain within this family, do you understand?" I look at each one of them.

In a flurry of agreement, they all answer "yes" then are quiet.

"When I first made the discovery, your mother and I sat down to discuss potential effects, both on our family and on our friends. We decided to keep it secret so it wouldn't run our lives."

"For heaven's sake Dad, just tell us what's going on." Angus says in angst.

"I've been gradually bringing back gold nuggets and ore from our property and putting it in a safe place. The time has come to bring it to light and begin making plans for its use." I put it in the simplest way I can but the silence afterward is deafening.

Then all my children begin at once; "Where did you find it? What plans? What do you mean by 'making plans'?"

I quiet them down, "I know you have lots of questions and I will answer as many as I can, but I think the eldest in the family should ask first and that's you Briana."

"Can we see it?" she asks. Angus and Kenna laugh at her question.

"It's a logical question and yes, you can see some of it right now." I pull three nuggets from my pocket, one for each of them and place them in the middle of the table. At first they stare at the gold but each finally picks one up, turning it over and feeling its weight. They've never seen gold, except in necklaces and rings on other people and they seem amazed to hold it in the palm of their hand.

"Does this mean we're rich?" Kenna asks quietly.

'Rich' is purely a person's point of view." I answer.

"Well in my point of view Dad, I think the answer is "yes." Angus says with a smile.

"Okay Angus, so noted. But as a father, I expect all of you to conduct yourselves with honor and respect for others in spite of this gift and never forget where our roots are.

"Consider this; if a fisherman has a good day's catch, or a farmer, a good lambing season, both feel fortunate; but what does a man out of work think about them both?" I pause to let them reflect, then continue.

"I know from previous life in Scotland, a man out of work would think both are very rich." Their faces indicate understanding and I continue.

"Think of this as a gift which gives each of us options for living our lives differently and requiring both planning and forethought. So I want you all included in the decisions to be made."

I tell them of my conversation with Ethan, as much as they need to know at this point and keep the hiding place under the floor a secret. I collect the nuggets so they won't be tempted to show their friends; I trust them, but they are children, not yet wise of the world and an early reveal would upset any control we have over the matter.

The next morning, I take our buggy to Ethan's and we ride into town to see Thomas. He's at the forge when we arrive and we wait until he finishes.

"Hello gentlemen, didn't expect to see you so early in the week, everything alright?"

"Yes it is." I say with a smile, "You have time to sit awhile?"

"What's going on?" He asks.

I hold up a nugget to him and he turns on his heel to put a "Back at Noon" sign up on his doors and latches them snugly.

"My journeyman isn't in this morning so we're alone in the shop." He wears a big grin on his face and grabs me in a bear hug saying "Are congratulations in order? How can I help?"

"We could do with the use of your scales for starters." Thomas's eyebrows shoot up.

"Of course; it's that good is it? Let's sit down and work out the particulars." We all sit down at a table in the corner of the shop where we talk and decide to bring separate, smaller loads of gold to weigh first before taking it on to the Bank.

I bring up a new subject for my friends, "I want to speak in confidence with a bank officer ahead of time;" "either of you have personal experience with one? I feel like I'm jumping off a cliff here." I laugh nervously.

"Well Daniel, I've always dealt with Samuel Sinclair since the town's bank opened." Ethan says, "He's been honest and straightforward and his personal ethics are good. You can't go wrong with going to the top and Sam is the current bank president here in the settlement."

"I agree," Thomas adds, "he's an honest man. He and his family come from the North Island, born and raised."

Since it's mid-week, I decide to go today to see Mr. Sinclair; maybe I can get in without an appointment I speculate. Ethan offers to come along but since it's almost noon, Thomas stays behind to open the shop.

The new bank is a modest-sized building with double doors. Gold lettering on the window states hours of operation and the artist even outlined the window with fancy curlicues at the corners like a big-city bank. The main room has two teller cages and a secretary outside the president's office.

"Is Mr. Sinclair in?" I ask at her desk and we are seated while she checks.

"Ethan, always good to see you." Mr. Sinclair extends his hand in greeting.

"Sam, its been a while. This is a good friend of mine, Daniel Smith, who has some business to conduct."

"Daniel, good to meet you; I believe you're one of our customers aren't you, I've seen you at the windows."

"We've had an account here since you opened Mr. Sinclair."

"Well, I appreciate your business. Please sit down, how can I help you today."

"I assume you buy gold?" I ask.

"Oh yes, we've rendered the service since the first discovery in Lawrence, though business is down with the west coast discoveries. Are you interested in investing?"

"Before we go on Mr. Sinclair, I want your assurance of complete confidentiality and whatever we discuss will go no further."

"Mr. Smith, I assure you whatever is said in this room today will be held to compliance with strict banking rules rendered by our main office in Wellington and in the United Kingdom; we take the subject very seriously."

"That's reassuring. I have a substantial amount of gold I wish to begin turning over for purchase."

"Very good news Mr. Smith, congratulations. Before we proceed, may I see a sample?"

"Of course," I place one of the larger nuggets on his desk in front of him and watch with humor as his eyes widen.

"My goodness." He remarks and immediately picks up the nugget to weigh it in his hand then turns to pick up a small assay scale behind him. We watch as he weighs.

"I make it at 12 ounces gentleman and alluvial which I would guess is anywhere from 93-97% pure if local. Of course the Assayer will need to do his tests for the official results, but samples of alluvial gold from this area tend to be in that range."

He replaces the scale behind him.

"Current gold price per troy ounce is £3.15s 11d. After mint and duty charges, this sample's value would be in the neighborhood of $38 dollars. My questions for you; how many pounds do you have to turn over and are they all alluvial, or do you have coarse gold as well?"

"I'm no expert on what constitutes 'coarse gold' sir, but the majority of the lot are nuggets, or as you say, alluvial. As to total weight, I'm not ready to state specifically, other than it's somewhere in the five-thousand pound range."

The figure surprised Ethan previously and Sam's face shows the same reaction. Silence follows, so I continue.

"I'll bring the gold in several small lots, perhaps beginning next week? I'll need your advisement on what amount can be safely handled at a time and how this process will work."

"I'd say four-hundred pounds per delivery would be best." Sam advises, "The assay staff will examine the ore and conduct tests to determine the purity of the gold. Alluvial nuggets are easier to assay than mixed ore which can include quartz-containing gold, pyrite, or other impurities including silver.

"The gold in its current makeup will be shipped to our smelting facility for initial weigh-in, firing and weighing again after impurities are removed. The price per ounce will be determined then duty and regular taxes will be subtracted from your final payment."

"How long will this assaying take?" I ask.

"We've opened our own assay and melting house on the west coast in Okarito and it operates quite efficiently. With time in transport to the other coast, either by ship or overland and depending upon their work load, I'd say no more than sixty days."

I take a moment to glance at Ethan who has no other questions to add. "Sam, I think you've answered my questions except for more specifics on how you want the gold delivered, container, that sort of thing."

"Of course, wait just a moment and I'll give you some written instructions to take along."

185

"Looks like we're on the way" Ethan says. "How do you feel?"

"Okay, I guess; still nervous about the whole thing. This is a heck of a lot harder than picking up nuggets." But I can laugh over the subject for the first time.

After we leave the office, I remember why I felt uneasy when Sam talked about transporting the gold to Okarita. Several ships went down on the way last winter and their cargo of gold ore was lost at sea.

"Do you think I should have specified how I wanted the gold delivered?" I ask.

Ethan looks over at me. "I think you're going to have to turn loose of it sooner or later Daniel. I know it's a heavy responsibility, but some things only the good Lord knows the outcome of and this is probably one of them."

Our last stop is the local attorney's office to make sure all bases are covered regarding the gold and its disbursement. Last night I realised I've never made a will and today my attorney draws one up with Ethan as a witness.

We return to fill in Thomas and make plans to weigh the first load this coming Monday. When I get home I'll call another family meeting to update the children.

"Today I want to repeat what I said during our first family meeting," I tell my youngsters, "it's extremely important to keep the gold secret a little while longer."

I have to trust they realise the seriousness of this before I enlist their help over the next few weeks. The girls are eighteen and Angus is seventeen; though they've known responsibility for the farm, but nothing as serious as the firestorm which could hit us now, should word get out.

"Ethan and I went to town today to discuss how we'll be selling the gold and how to get it from here to the Bank." I watch their faces question the word "here" but I stop their questions for the moment.

"We have to agree now on secrecy before I can continue. I'd like each of your oaths you will keep this matter only between us. Briana, would you bring your Mother's Bible over here please?" When the Bible lays on the table, I ask each of them to lay their right hand on it.

"I'm not experienced in making up formal words, so I will say as clearly as possible what I need from you all and you repeat after me: "I do solumnly swear...I will keep in confidence....any and all information concerning our family's gold.... I will not use the gold in conversation outside our family....or answer any questions asked outside our family...so help me God." And when the last word is spoken and echoed around the table, their faces are solemn and I feel they're ready.

"You must have heard and read some of the theft and robbery going on in the gold fields by now. I don't want you to be afraid, but I want you to take no chances by letting clues slip we may have gold on the premises, or are going to transport it into town. I'm satisfied all of you realise the importance of the oath, but do you have any questions?"

"Dad, where is the gold?" Angus asks.

"Right under your nose." I answer then walk over to the area left of the fireplace.

"Your Mother and I started storing it under the floor here where I stand when you were all just babies. Angus, fetch me a shovel outside the door please. Girls, can you move this rug?"

In short order the braided rug is rolled up and moved away, the shovel finds a crack between the granite pavers and several are soon pulled out of place and put aside.

"Angus, open the lid and pull out a sample."

He does as told and sits back on his heels to look at two nuggets in his hands, both heavy and white, coated with the stream's mineral deposits. He sees some color show through and looks to me in amazement.

"Now you know why we felt it best not to discuss the gold all these years. We didn't want its weight and influence on our growing family and kept it only as a back-up for our future. You've all grown up with fine values and you're not afraid to work hard for what you want. I honestly couldn't ask for more and I know your mother feels the same, wherever she is."

I walk away saying, "Replace those stones Angus and we'll get on with this." Out of their sight, I wipe my eyes roughly remembering my Rose and how excited and surprised she'd been when I brought the first nugget to her.

When we're all seated again, I tell them my plan.

"Ethan, Thomas and I have decided to weigh one load a week at Thomas' shop before delivery to the Bank. We'll use small shipping containers from Anderson's for the load, to save time and money on crating."

"We estimate it will take about twelve weeks to complete the deliveries and we'll change days and times so we don't show a pattern. We'll take care of all that, beginning Monday, if you'll help load it up. Any questions?"

"Do you want me to ride with you Dad?"

"Angus, thanks for volunteering but I need you here at home to take care of your sisters and the farm while I'm gone."

The room falls silent for a moment. Kenna asks "Dad, does this mean I can go to university?" Her eyes shine with excitement.

"Well I think it's a reasonable expectation." My heart swells with pride.

"Yes, it is possible and not just for Kenna, but for you Angus and you Briana." They look at each other and gradually the smiles come.

"I know this is a lot for each of you to take in, but I want to tell you my personal plan so you have plenty of time to think about it.

"Your mother and I used to talk about the families we left behind in Scotland and our childhood memories. Conditions were bad when we left; wars, people struggling to find work, lack of food and the desperation of the land, but though some still suffer, Aberdeen has come full circle and the economy has recovered well." I proceed to tell them the part I'm most worried about telling them.

"You probably never knew I worked as a granite cutter in Scotland's quarries. I started raising sheep with your grandfather to keep food on the table and used the experience to get started here. But my mind has always been back with the granite...and I want to purchase a granite quarry and build my own business...in Scotland." I pause to see what impact my words will have on them.

"Dad, you mean you'd move back to Scotland?" Angus asks.

"Yes, that's right son."

"But what about the farm and all the work we've done?"

"And what about the gold Dad, do you think there's more?" Briana asks.

"The farm is dear to me Angus because your mother and I made our life here. We took something miserably broken down and brought it way past what Mr. and Mrs. Riley could do. It's an accomplishment I'm proud of and I'm not too old to pursue yet another dream. Understand though, I don't expect you to change your dreams because of me."

Angus turns to look at Briana and Kenna, realizing they will all have to make decisions for themselves.

191

"Briana, I don't know the answer to your question about 'more gold'. If so, it may require heavy equipment and contracting a mining company to work it for us, but Ethan, Thomas and I will sit down together soon and perhaps I'll have more answers.

"Most important is that we stay solid as a family and don't get at odds with each other over this. Whatever our personal decisions about the future, we'll talk often during the next few weeks and none of you need be afraid to ask or let me know truthfully how you feel." I pause and they seem to look at me with understanding.

"I love you all very much and will not make any decisions without you, that's a promise. Now, let's get cleaned up for dinner and leave these discussions for now. Angus, help me feed the stock."

I follow Dad out to the barn. The sun is beginning to set beyond the bay at the western ridge and the sky is pink and gray. The sheep gather together for sleep in the pasture and I look at the scene with new eyes.

What's it like in Scotland I wonder. Our work here is hard and I know it like the back of my hand. Can I face a new beginning as Dad did so many years ago? I have to decide in the weeks ahead because right now, I just don't have an answer.

Chapter 8   Well-laid Plans

This Sunday afternoon my children and I work to load our first four hundred pounds of nuggets and coarse gold on the wagon. We bring it by bucket from the house to the 3x6x4 foot crate I've lined with oil cloth so any residual flakes can be recovered after unloading. Looking at the completed load, I recognize it's a symbol of our new beginning and this day will be long remembered.

I ride out early for Ethan's, unworried about trouble with this load as no one will be expecting it with just a few isolated nuggets and dust found in the hill country. I'll pick up Ethan, knowing at the very least he'll have a shotgun.

Sure enough, he's waiting on the porch and walks to the wagon with coffee cup in one hand and a shotgun in the other.

"Mornin." He puts the gun in the foot well and climbs up the side to his seat. "Ready for this?"

"Ready as I'll ever be." I give the reins a light snap, setting Sister in motion toward town.

We arrive uneventfully at Thomas's shop and pull the wagon into the main part of the barn so he can close and bar the doors behind us.

"I kept one of the crates here I picked up last week and weighed it empty." Thomas says. "This morning we'll hook your loaded crate to the overhead pulley and drop it on the scales and subtract the known weight of the crate. You agree?"

Ethan nods and I say, "Let's do it."

We help hook up the crate and do the weigh-in. After our calculations we find a weight of 398 pounds 10 ounces and stand silent for a moment.

"With the price of gold, it means approximately $25,000 dollars is sitting here in front of us." Thomas says.

"Course, that'll be something less after its melted down." I add.

"And don't forget the tax." Ethan reminds me.

"Still a good return for one load." Thomas says and we all stand up, unable to sit still. Smiles break out and we bask in the knowledge better days are ahead.

Ethan and I pull the wagon behind the Bank per Sam Sinclair's directions and knock at the livery door where his horse and buggy are kept. The livery is spacious so we pull in and close the doors behind us.

Sam comes to greet us with two security men in uniform who unload the crate from the wagon with a rope pulley.

"Impressive." He says and bends over to pick up several nuggets. "Congratulations Daniel." He offers a firm handshake, "If this is any example of what the rest is like, you have nothing to worry about."

"Glad to hear it, Sam." I feel relieved as I follow him inside. Ethan stays with the horse and plans to watch how the gold is handled and secured until its disposition.

"Come into my office, we'll get some papers signed and get this process started."

"Mr Sinclair, I haven't told anyone of this find or its location except my own attorney here in town. He directed me to give you this letter and papers, it should be all you need to proceed. The safety of my family is first and foremost and I won't have anything jeopardizing them."

"Understood Daniel and I can offer complete confidentiality on the part of myself and my staff. The men you saw outside are bonded couriers and work for the Bank. Your name will not be known as the gold passes to the assayers and the furnace. I can even assign a false name, if you wish; the only record would be here in my safe and of course made known to you in a sealed envelope."

"I like the sound of that. Also, I'd like to set up a delivery date for next week on a different day, perhaps Wednesday? I want to keep the days and times varied, so it won't be easy for someone to figure out."

"This facility has been receiving gold for years with only one robbery in this town as a result of, shall we say, a relaxing of security on a private storage facility our predecessors owned. We've brought storage here now and I can assure you, the vault is sturdy and guarded. We of course, use an armed and bonded escort to deliver gold to the furnace and assayer."

"I appreciate the reassurance; this is my family's future we're handling." At this point, one of the men from the livery enters the office to deliver a piece of paper to him.

"I quite agree Daniel. Now here's your receipt for the shipment, I've signed it and noted the weight received as just now reported; 398 pounds and 9 ounces."

"It almost matches the weight we found an hour ago, 398 pounds and 10 ounces. One ounce can be a big difference in terms of gold, don't you agree?"

"Certainly can and it's a concern. Can we agree to see what the next shipment brings? If it's also off an ounce, we'll have the scale's calibration checked. If it's deemed accurate, may I suggest you advise the owner of your scales of his equipment's discrepancy?"

"Fair enough." I fold the receipt and deposit it inside my coat. "Good day to you Sam, see you next week."

"I look forward to it." he answers.

As we ride home, I fill in Ethan on my conversation with Sam and he describes what he saw in the livery.

"It looks like everything is regimented and done according to written guidelines issued by the bank." Ethan tells me. "The men are professionals, there was no awkwardness in the way they secured this shipment and a 24/7 armed guard is posted. I think they'll do all they can to protect it."

"I hope so, I can't worry after it's out of my hands and have plenty to keep me busy with the rest of it. I can tell you, it'll be a load off my shoulders when the last crate is delivered and this is done."

❧ঌ

I put down my cup and stare briefly out the kitchen window at the increasing light across our fields. This morning marks our twelfth and last load. I sit in the quietness of the kitchen as the girls are just stirring upstairs and Angus already works in the barn.

I consciously push down the apprehension in my stomach, a routine occurrence on delivery days. Ethan's mentioned the same thing happens to him.

We're now getting attention from the townspeople who know us and it's pretty evident our pulling into the livery of the Bank is not a service offered to most customers. It's only a matter of time before word gets around to the wrong people.

I'm at Ethan's house as the sun breaks over the crest; it's Thursday morning; *last morning for this* I think.

He and I share a cup of coffee on the front porch then climb into the wagon. It rained last night, the road is muddy and I feel lucky no more streams need crossing. Ours was higher than normal on the way here, but Sister kept her footing and we came across safe and sound.

"Last trip." I remark as Ethan watches the road ahead.

"That it is my friend and I won't lie, this bumpy old wagon will not be missed by me." he laughs.

Kenna and I work to restore the house to its liveable condition now that Dad left earlier for Ethan's. He and Angus filled in the floor's excavation and reset the pavers last evening after we loaded the last of the ore.

"Thank Heaven." I say as we finish sweeping the floor then replace the rug in front of the fireplace.

"How wonderful not to have the mess in this room anymore." I flop into a rocker, "I'd forgotten what the room looks like when it's all clean and tidy. I can't believe Mum and Dad were able to put all of it under the floor without our catching on."

"Briana, we were in school, think about it. For hours everyday they could deposit the gold and clean up before we came home."

"You're right, I hadn't thought about that." We rock in silence for a few moments then I add, "I'm really going to miss this house when we leave."

"You've reached a decision then?" Kenna asks.

"I'm no good at being independent, you know. I'll go where the family goes and if it's Scotland, so be it. Have you decided what you want to do?"

"Yes, I want to go with Dad too and see where our parents both grew up. I also want to go to a university with more than ten students. Have you talked to Angus yet?" Kenna asks.

"No and he hasn't volunteered anything either. I want us all together, to marry, have children, be aunts and uncles, visit and see to Dad as he gets older. I don't like the idea of having any one of us more than five miles away."

"But you know Angus is the oldest and an only son; he can decide to stay and run the farm if he wants, it's just how it is."

❧

Less than halfway to town, Ethan and I see the rider come from the brush alongside the road at the same time. Ethan unconsciously reaches down for his shotgun but lets his hand rest on the gun's butt when the man yells "Hold it right there."

He rides his horse in front of Sister with gun drawn then shoots it into the air over our heads.

I pull back on the reins and Sister dances as the wagon presses her forward with its momentum until she can finally stop.

"What's this all about?" I yell, preparing for a fight.

The man sneers at me, "It's about why you two have been riding to town every week mister." He keeps his revolver aimed and ready to fire as he approaches the side of the wagon. "Kinda strange anyone'd visit the bank so often."

When I hear his remark, I know he's been watching for some weeks and has a plan. We're between farms at this point, far enough away no one will hear the man's gunshot and near enough to the crossroads north where he can drive the wagon into the hills before we get help. Or worse, he can leave us both wounded or dead in the bushes. It would be days before anyone found us and the rain would leave no clues in the muddy road. All of this flashes through my mind in a few seconds and I know I have to do something, but what?

He rides by Ethan to the rear of the wagon and lifts the canvas covering the crate.

"Well, well" he feigns surprise. "You certainly have a lot of whatever it is in this box. How about you both climb down nice and slow and come back here."

It's an order, not an invitation and Ethan looks at me. I have a feeling if we do what he asks, neither of us will be getting back on the wagon. I wink at Ethan and begin to tie off the reins.

"Come on, get down now." the man yells, waving his gun at us.

At Daniel's wink I prepare myself and move cautiously. Dan suddenly changes the speed of his movement and jumps wide and far off the wagon. The man taken by surprise, fires off a couple of shots at Daniel who lands in a heap and doesn't move. As the shots echo down the valley the man fails to notice I'm holding a shotgun and the first shell is already his.

Everything goes quiet for what seems longer but he falls to the ground in less than a second and his horse runs away. I watch to make sure he's no longer a threat then look to the other side of the wagon where Daniel lays in the mud. Awkwardly, still holding the shotgun, I climb down to my friend.

He's face-down and I carefully roll him over to see where he's shot. The blood all over his forehead makes me fear the worst and I mop some of it away with a clean kerchief.

"It's a crease my friend, doesn't look too serious." The relief I feel makes the words catch in my throat.

"Easy for you to say." I hear Daniel whose eyes are still closed. "Just let me lie here for a minute and get my bearings, okay?"

"Okay, but don't take all day, we still have a delivery to make." I try to act nonchalant but my hand is a little shaky as I try to put my hat under Daniel's head gently then get up to take a look at the robber.

The man is wounded, bleeding from a deep shoulder wound and groaning in pain. He looks to be in his late thirties, unwashed and unshaven.

"You may not believe it now but you're lucky you weren't further away." I say as I tear the man's shirt and stuff the rag into the wound.

"The new munitions make a bigger hole the longer the distance to entry and as far as I'm concerned, you missed your fair share."

I stow the man's gun in the front of the wagon then return to pull him up and deposit him unceremoniously in the back beside the crate.

"You get a free ride to visit the Constable, oh and be careful, this crate is four-hundred pounds and tends to slide a little on these muddy roads."

By the time I've finished in the back, Daniel's sitting up and holding his forehead. I tie one of Jane's ironed handerkerchiefs over the wound.

"Come on, let's get you into the wagon." Somehow I'm able to half-drag him up onto the seat and get Sister pointed the right direction to town. It's a rough ride before we pull up in front of the Constable's office.

Constable Robert Guerin looks out his window, grabs a pistol and meets me as I climb down from the wagon. People on the street crowd around to see what's going on.

"What happened?" Guerin asks as he helps me get Daniel down from the wagon.

"Get the doctor over here." I bark at a citizen, who immediately runs to the other side of the street to fetch him and I look back to the Constable.

"Got a present for you in the back of the wagon. He came out of the bush along the upper road, discharged his pistol at us and tried to steal our wagon." I sit Daniel on the steps of the jail before continuing.

"He was ready to shoot us both when my friend here jumped wide from the wagon to distract him and I got a shot off. His shoulder's pretty bad but he'll probably make it to stand trial."

The Constable and his deputy haul the robber into the building and leave him on a bed rack.

After locking the cell, they return outside to find the doc already examining Daniel's wound.

"Let's get him over to my office so I can clean this up. He's a lucky man, another inch and he'd be in much worse shape."

"Doc, we'll need you to take a look at the prisoner too when you finish with Mr. Smith," the Constable directs then turns to me.

"One of you needs to complete a report Ethan, if you want this man to stand trial. You can come over after you finish; I'll be here."

"Appreciate it Robert; I have to take this wagon to the Bank first then stop to see how Daniel's doing."

"It's early, we have all day."

"You don't know how good that sounds. We came near to losing all our options earlier." I exhale then and climb back in the wagon to finish the delivery.

⁂

It's been a long day in town and it's almost five o'clock when we return to Ethan's. My head is throbbing from the bullet's graze and we're both beginning to feel the aftershock of the day as weariness starts to settle in but Ethan refuses to rest until we see his Scot's flag. After we reach his farm, he caves a bit at James' urging and allows him to drive us the rest of the way to my place in the buggy.

When my children see me at the door with my head wrapped up and leaning on James, they react as I knew they would.

"Dad. What happened?" Angus shouts and they all attempt to help me the rest of the way in.

Ethan comes from behind saying "We had a little meeting with a robber on the road, but believe me, he's in much worse shape than your Dad." James makes Ethan sit while he answers their questions.

When at last everyone has calmed down, Angus helps me to the loft and settles me in bed. Kenna brings some hot soup with fresh-baked bread and feels relieved when I finish it up in short order.

"Now you stay in bed, you hear me? I don't want to see you up until tomorrow." Her tone softens, "Glad you're home Dad."

"You and me both my daughter."

James and Ethan are preparing to leave when Kenna returns downstairs.

"Thanks for bringing him home safe Uncle Ethan." She gives him a hug as does Briana and even Angus adds a hug to his handshake saying, "We're indebted to you Ethan."

"Nothing a friend wouldn't do." Ethan says and turns to James, "Let's get home before you have to put me in a potato sack for the night."

James calls to me from the wagon as I stand in the doorway. "Angus, let us know if you need anything tomorrow, okay?"

"I will." I answer and watch them pull away.

My sisters return inside, but I linger a moment to soak in the quiet of the night and say a silent 'thanks' to God.

It's dark of the moon and I can just make out the orange tree's outline a few feet from the house. An owl breaks the peace with its cry and I think there's a shadow near the tree, but when I look closer it's gone. I step back into the house to close and lock the door.

✍✍

After breakfast and a bandage change, I'm surprised to hear a knock at the door. When I open it, John Rogers the Circuit Court judge, stands on the doorstep.

"Daniel Smith? I'm Judge Rogers, here on business for the territory's circuit court. I wonder if I might have an hour of your time this morning, if you feel up to it after your injuries yesterday?"

"Of course Sir. It's an honor to meet you. But how did you know?"

"I talked with Constable Guerin briefly this morning. I'm in town on an unscheduled visit, passing through on my way back to Wellington.

"Robert told me of your injury and I talked to the prisoner as well. Looks like he's going to be in shape for trial, so I thought it would be simpler to stop by your farm on the way for your testimomy instead of requiring your presence at the jail."

"I appreciate it your Honor. Please sit down; can I get you anything?"

"A drink of water would be fine. Any chance your friend Ethan Shepherd is nearby?"

"He's at his farm, but his son James is here working. I can ask him to fetch him."

"I hate to do it after yesterday's events, but yes if he can come over, it would serve to move things along."

"Should take a little less than an hour to get him back here." I summon James from the barn and he leaves quickly.

While we wait, the Judge relates what he knows of the culprit.

"The man who shot you is an Irish prisoner sentenced to labour through the English courts and brought to Port Phillip, New Wales. We believe he left unauthorized as part of a ship's crew to Auckland and eventually started south, perhaps drawn by the gold discoveries.

"He was up to no good all along the coast; robbery of goods, petty theft, until he killed a man in Wellington last spring. That's when we began pursuing him."

"So he's not opposed to killing for what he wants." Not a question I think, but a statement of fact.

"It's apparent you and your friend are very lucky Mr. Smith."

"I have no doubts your Honor."

"Multiple charges will be entered, including murder and your attempted murder; I'll probably set the trial for early summer. In the meantime I'll have him transferred under guard to Wellington for safe keeping. I'd like to know you and Ethan will be on hand to testify."

"I see no reason why we wouldn't be and I want to see this through."

Ethan arrives and after he's brought up to date, we both assure the Judge we'll be in Wellington as soon as notified by the Constable.

❧

The trial yields conviction on all charges and a generous reward is offered to Ethan and me for the robber's apprehension. We talk it over and decide to donate the money to the Church to build a new Hall.

We attach the only condition, that both our wives' graves be taken care of in perpetuity, after our immediate families are gone. Pastor Bush assures us with a written note entered to the Church's record this morning then surprises us with something else.

"We voted last night at our regular business meeting to dedicate the Hall to the service of the needy. We'd like to name it "Rose and Catherine's" after your two lovely wives."

"Rose would be so humbled by your gesture Pastor." I tell him.

"Likewise Pastor, Catherine would be happy to see her "orphans" as she called them, are taken care of." Ethan adds.

"Our sincere thanks to you both on behalf of our members." Pastor Bush continues, "In their days with us, both women were committed to helping the needy and now they will not be forgotten."

❧❧

In less than two months, I receive word from Sam Sinclair he's ready to meet with me at the bank. I still experience memories of the robbery but they serve to remind me I'm blessed to be here today.

I decide to take Angus, Briana and Kenna along so they can share the excitement and tell the story to their children someday. So, on this unusually warm day in late September I park the buggy and help the girls to the sidewalk while Angus ties off Sister then we walk in together.

To the secretary I say, "Daniel Smith and family to see Mr. Sinclair, he's expecting us." Through his open door I hear "Daniel. Come in, please"

He comes around his desk to meet us. "Please, introduce me to your lovely family."

"Of course; this is Kenna and her sister Briana and my son Angus."

"Wonderful to meet you all." He shakes each of their hands and offers chairs.

"How are you Daniel? No lasting effect after your assault I hope?"

"No sir, I'm perfectly fine, but I do have this to show for it" I brush my hair aside to show the three inch, horizontal scar left by the bullet's passing.

"Bully. Glad it's the only souvenir of the occasion. On another note, I have good news Daniel, your gold is 98.6 percent pure and it means you received a less than two percent cut for impurities per ounce."

"That's really good isn't it?"

211

"Yes, its 'really good' Daniel and this is what we've deposited into your account after duty and taxes." He hands me an envelope over the desk.

When I open it, everyone leans in to read the paper. It's a deposit slip in an amount over £394,504s.

I smile as both Briana and Kenna show their surprise. Angus exhibits amazement while Sam watches the scene with enjoyment.

"Thank-you Sam for all your support through this ordeal." Then I realize I'm probably shaking his hand longer than is proper.

"You're very welcome Daniel. Let me wish you all the best in the future after your hard work."

"Thank-you. I'm not much of a miner and probably won't be again but this experience has taught me a lot besides patience and faith. There is such a thing as a new beginning but most importantly, you can't count on it to go the way you plan it; only God has the one real plan."

"Wise words, Daniel. Now if you'd like to talk more about future investments or financial planning, I'd be honored to assist in any way I can."

"I may take you up on it when the time is right."

We say our goodbyes and walk out to the buggy.

"Dad, can we have a family meeting when we get home?" Angus asks.

"Yes son, absolutely."

I drive the buggy out the main street, watching the stores which have sprung up since we first walked this dusty little town. Fixed sidewalks now, no more puddles to skip over when it rains and the vertible river flowing down the street during rainy season has been averted. The 'Soup Kitchen' closed years ago when Muriel decided to retire and return to England. The old Land Office building was razed and in its place, a larger building stands, a tailor shop and shoe repair run by my old friends George and Mary Strickland with their son Joseph. The town that thrived during the gold rush days has quieted down to a new-normal life style and commerce. The Church has grown and Pastor Bush continues to serve with the help of his son William who finished seminary last year.

"Dad...Dad?" Kenna nudges me, "Where are you?"

"You caught me. I'm just thinking of all the changes I've seen here since your mother and I followed James and his goat cart up a narrow, dusty two-rut road."

"A goat cart...you're joking aren't you?" Briana says. "Why would you do such a thing?"

"He had a need to make money and we needed our trunks transported – simple."

I laugh at the memory then say, "Let me tell you about our first night," and I tell the story as I guide Sister safely back to the farm amidst their laughter.

Chapter 9 Miles

I sit on a bench under the shade of the orange tree with my drawing paper. It's officially summer and Kenna and I celebrate our birthdays today.

Dad gave us both "the day off" from chores and invited all our family's friends for dinner tonight. So I've chosen to use my time-off on my favorite thing and draw pictures of this farm I love.

Over the years I've filled several books with charcoal drawings; the barn and its contents, the animals, the old pump, the inside of our home, some of the wild insects and beetles in the field and even one of Dad. But with all the talk about leaving, I realise I've never drawn the front of our home, so it's my subject today.

Dad returns from town and waves from the buggy as he drives in.

"Dad, what have you been doing?" I ask innocently, knowing he's been purchasing something for our special day.

"Just never you mind," he calls from the buggy with a smile, "it's a secret."

"Oh Dad, I'm eighteen, well past all that. Just tell me."

"Nope." It's his final answer as he continues on to the back of the house and calls over his shoulder, "And don't come inside for another half-hour."

"Yes Dad." I answer and go back to my drawing.

❧

After entering by the kitchen door, I make two trips upstairs with packages for the girls, covering them with a blanket beside my bed.

The last package I leave downstairs in the cupboard for safekeeping until tonight's party. With three inquisitive grown children, it's next to impossible to surprise anyone, but I'm sure going to try.

I walk Sister out to the barn to see what Angus is doing and find him putting up feed and cleaning the barn.

"Good job son." I say as I take the traces off Sister and tie her to a post.

"No problem, you've got your hands full with preparations and I'm pretty clear for the day." He picks up the brushes to give Sister a going-over before turning her out to the pasture. "You find everything you wanted in town?"

"Sure did and probably more than I should have; some of the merchants are cutting their inventory and prices are good. But you'll see tonight."

I watch my father walk back to the house. The change in him the last few weeks is surprising. He's been more withdrawn each year but with the weight of finances now lifted and the hope of a new life in Scotland, he seems happier. His enthusiasm in family and friends is back and it makes a difference in our home life.

At eighteen, I think I now understand what it took for Dad to continue with the farm after Mum's death.

I ask myself, as I have many times over the past months, is this what I want for my life, *shall I stay?* I have friends from school, but not 'good' friends, just acquaintances really. New Zealand is my home, but what about the rest of the world out there?

For some reason at this moment, I realise I want to see it. *So that's how it is.* I smile to myself and know my decision is made.

This evening I've invited Ethan, Jane, Michael and James to the girl's birthday dinner, as well as Thomas, George and Mary Strickland with their son Joseph.

Every lamp in the house is lit and I take a lamb roast out of the oven which I cooked, having given the girls the day off. I set it on the table with carving knives beside it; next come young potatoes in cream, some early asparagus and a fresh loaf of bread. Not bad I say to myself as I give the table a final lookover.

"Come on everyone, let's sit down." I call, taking the makeshift apron-towel off my belt.

They don't need to be called twice and respond to the enticing aromas from the table. I look around at my friends and family with good feelings but also with some measure of sadness knowing soon we'll all be far away from them. I include in the saying of grace, a special blessing on everyone who sits with us tonight.

"Dad, if I'd known you cooked this well, you would have been relegated to the kitchen more often." Kenna jokes.

"You think so little girl? Remember I am your father and what I say goes." I chide her and everyone laughs, knowing either one of the girls can wrap me around their little fingers at will.

"I want to propose a toast to my fine son and to these beautiful young women who as you can tell, take after their mother. Through the years this family has worked hard together to make this farm successful. Angus, my son, I look to you to carry the family name into whatever you decide to do in life and I am well satisfied with you, so far." Everyone smiles at my little joke.

"My daughters took on responsibilities they shouldn't have had at their young ages, but they've done a fine job of it and I know they will make a success of anything they decide to do in their lives; School, careers, running a house, raising children. They've put up with me haven't they? A toast to your very happy birthdays, Briana and Kenna." Everyone lifts their glass to the girls and plates are passed, some more than once as we all enjoy each other's company.

When the meal is a pleasant memory and everyone has pushed back from the table, Jane and James clear the dishes. I slip upstairs and return with two packages wrapped in brown paper and tied with ribbon. Next I retrieve the cake from the cupboard which I ordered at the new bakery in town. It's fancier than anything I could make, probably more edible and covered in pink sugar roses with ribbons around its sides. The girls see it and exclaim "Dad. It's wonderful."

Before dessert, our guests walk outside for some fresh air and to stretch their legs in the gathering twilight.

Within a few minutes though, Ethan glances across the yard and sees a shadow of someone standing at the barn. He asks the guests to return inside and calls me to the door.

I suspect it might be Teki as he is overdue for his usual visit. Angus told me he saw someone in the front yard the evening of the robbery, which may have been Tiki.

He comes closer upon seeing me and I notice he's really changed since our last meeting. His hair is gray and he leans on the walking stick more than in years past.

"Good evening sirs" he says to me and Ethan.

"Teki." I say, but before I can say more, the old native asks "Your young ones are well?"

"Yes they are, thank-you."

"These for women to wear." He extends his open hand toward me and two rings made from the green stone lay inside.

"These are beautiful, but wouldn't you like to give them to the girls yourself? Please, come in and sit with us."

He's never come inside over the years, but now walks with me to the doorway then hesitates. Again I say, "please come in" and he steps through the door.

The guests are surprised and a little wary at his appearance, but it is Angus who steps forward first.

"Welcome Teki to our home." He extends his hand and it's taken by the old man and shaken strongly.

"Good evening" the old man says to each person as they offer their hands, too.

I bring a bench from the fireside for him and hand him the rings back, saying "for you to present to the girls" and he nods.

After everyone wishes the girls a happy birthday, the cake is cut and served with coffee. Teki eats his piece with gusto and smiles his approval then rises to present the rings to Kenna and Briana. They are thrilled and put them on to show him they fit, then thank him. Seeming satisfied, he turns to me.

"I will not see you again my friend. May the spirit guide you in your travels always." He offers his hand and I grip it firmly in friendship. His eyes meet mine and I am reminded again of our first meeting so many years ago on the wharf.

He turns to leave quietly through the kitchen door, as his words continue to echo in my mind.

Gifts are being opened when I turn from the door and when the girls see the surprises inside the boxes, they both gasp.

Each receives a beautiful new dress specially made for them from Mary Strickland's dress shop. Briana's is a coral-color silk with lace at the cuffs and neckline and Kenna's is a pale blue silk, with white tatting trim.

"Come by if you need alterations, no extra charge." Mary tells them. "Oh, I think you'll both look lovely. One thing I've missed is having daughters to sew for."

I draw two small boxes from my pocket and hand one to each.

"Oh Dad," Kenna says as she sees the earrings to match the blue of her dress, each a single blue saphire sparkling in a gold setting. Briana's are white saphires in silver settings because I think they match the sparkle in her eyes.

After both come to hug me, they excuse themselves and disappear upstairs to try on their new dresses.

Angus, Michael, Joseph and James sit down to play a game of chinese checkers while the rest of us have some coffee.

"Well folks, we need to start back to town." George says at last. "The dinner was delicious; we've really enjoyed ourselves."

Mary agrees, "It's just been so nice to see you all before you start your new adventure. We will miss you; and you have to write, promise Daniel?"

"I will make it a habit at least twice a year Mary. And Joseph, you continue to take care of your folks, as I know you will."

"Thank-you all for coming." I watch them get into their buggy and drive away before closing the door.

"Daniel," Ethan says, "you once asked if I'd be interested in buying the farm and doing some mining."

"That's right, have you thought it over?" I help myself to more cake.

"We have." He nods to Jane and James at the table.

"We'd like to give it a try and James wants to try his hand at farming."

"Hold on there, don't forget me." Thomas pipes up, "Smithing is a good living, but I might make a good miner, too."

"We've never had trouble planning strategies," Ethan says, "and I think we can handle being in business together."

"You're right about that." I agree. "Let's meet later this week and work out the details. I've been thinking of a name for the gold mine; tell me what you think.

"Because we're friends, I thought maybe a symbolic name would be appropriate, something we can use in communication regarding the mine since I won't be here.

"I've found a seashell signifies good luck in some indian cultures of the world. What do you say, the Shell Mine? Secret meaning would be The Good Luck Mine? Think about it until we meet next week and tell me what you decide."

A few weeks later, we have an addendum written to the farm sale contract between Ethan, Thomas and myself and name the Shell Mine. I ordered brass seals made for each of us in the shape of a seashell and we use it for the first time to emboss the contract.

We'll all be equal partners in any gold revenue from the mine, but annual profit for the farm itself will go to James per our original agreement.

James surprisingly intends to run the farm and live here. He's content to be a 'country gentleman' as he calls himself, even though he's finished his classes and will continue in a two year internship in town with my attorney, Heinrich Moser.

"Imagine, I'll have a son who's a lawyer. What if Michael decides to follow?" I remark to Jane when we talk over the day's events at home.

"Ethan, it's not going to happen, he's going to be a doctor some day." Jane throws a stubborn look at me.

"Either calling is really fine," I reply, "and I'll be proud no matter what our children decide."

"I know that, you great galoot" she says and pulls me back for a hug. "I'm just teasing you."

There's a glint of mischief in her eyes. "What are you up to?" I ask.

"Well Ethan, in case you do want two lawyers in the family, we're getting another chance in about six months."

"My dear, are you sure? How did this happen?"

"Well, I imagine it happened in the usual manner sir, are you happy about it?"

"Of course I'm happy, it's a miracle!"

February arrives with lots of rain and wind. Dad and I keep busy seeing to the sheep and isolate most to the fields furthest from the stream as it swells and overflows its banks for several days. We're very thankful the house is out of reach.

When the storm finally passes and we are able to better assess the damage, we find the barn has withstood the wind but the feed is wet and without salvage. It will be several days before a trip into town can be made because of the stream which still runs fast over the road. Until it can be safely forded, Sister, our cows and fowl will have to be content with what they gleen from the land.

❧❧

Briana and Kenna meet me for a secret talk one day while Dad's in town and we decide unanimously to go with him to Scotland.

"You realise this is probably the first time we've all three agreed on the same thing in our lives?" I remark to my sisters.

"But Angus, it's about the rest of our lives and Dad's new life isn't it." Kenna speaks up. "He's given up so much for us all, it's time we were supportive of him."

"I agree," Briana says in her usual cheerful way, "It's our turn to be there for him, in whatever way we can. This isn't going to be easy for any of us, but together I think we'll be fine. You tell him tonite, Angus, okay?"

This evening I bring a pitcher of milk to the table for dinner and wear a rather sad face which is directly opposite of my feelings.

"Dad, we have something to tell you."

"What is it son?"

"We've talked over going to Scotland and we've come to a decision..." I draw out the pause and glance sideways at the girls.

"We've decided..."and my sisters join in, "to go with you." Dad seems to freeze momentarily when we finish.

"Dad? Are you alright?"

It's what I hoped and prayed for, but for just a second I wonder *are they doing it just for me?* I've prepared myself for the worst and instead they've all surprised me by joining together.

"It's what I hoped for," I declare, "and I love you all for your decision, but please don't do this just for me. It must feel right for you all as well."

"Dad," Angus says, "I don't think you realise what we've all known through the years; you are a good father. You get things done and perform miracles all the time with no fanfare or announcement, you just go ahead and do what's needed. I'm not ready to stop learning from you and intend to continue this journey with you."

Briana gets up from her chair and walks around the table to me.

"You've been all that to me as well Dad. We're not done yet and therefore we go with you."

"Where you are is home to us Dad, you're not getting rid of us just yet." Kenna joins Briana at my side.

"In that case, I welcome your decisions – now can we eat?" I joke as I swallow the lump in my throat.

We barely notice the meal as we make our plans and compile lists of things to do before leaving and it's a wonderful night.

With so much to do, I find time to meet with Sam Sinclair and arrange for my finances to be transferred to the Royal Bank of Scotland in Aberdeen.

He and I also take care of something special, a fund for the family of my friend Teki, with Ethan as administrator. The intent is to gift the money without making it seem like charity, which they would never accept. Ethan will find a way to make the occasional gift look like a random windfall for Teki's two sons and grand children and I know he'll handle it well, passing the responsibility on to James when the time comes.

❧

We are to set sail on a clipper barque for London in late September when the weather is tamer and seas calmer. My children have never been at sea and I worry about the girls, remembering how Rose suffered on the journey down.

I'm encouraged though when the agent shows me a drawing of the ship. It's a beautiful design, built in London and much sleeker than the tall ship, designed for fast delivery of cargo.

Its passenger cabins are for those who can afford to pay well and the girls will have their own cabin next door to Angus and me. Much more comfortable than the emigration ship Rose and I endured with total strangers in a cargo hold below decks.

Our time at sea is expected to be shorter and in sixty to seventy days barring bad weather, we should be arriving in London.

When all preparations and our to-do lists are complete, Angus and I load the wagon with the family's trunks then stand in the front yard with Briana and Kenna to take one last look at our farm.

I break the silence; "I remember how this house looked when your mother and I first drove up. She stood right about here and said it had 'possibilities'. Ethan and I started laughing because it looked so bad; the roof — gone; the entire yard overgrown with weeds and vines clear to the top of the walls. The chimney had a huge tree limb in it, the well was dry and the barn had rotted away along with most of the fence posts.

"The picture of the Riley's hung inside; your Mother imagined how bad they would feel if they saw it in such disrepair and vowed to make it right.

"Ethan, James and Thomas took pity on us and together we worked to get it liveable again." I reach to put my arms around the shoulders of my girls, who stand rather forlornly, tears in their eyes.

"I know this is hard to do; it's the only home you've known. I look at it and it links me to your mother, but its all right in here," I point to my heart, "and in all of yours, too. Take satisfaction in knowing we leave it in James' and Ethan's good care."

I kiss the girls on their foreheads and pull Angus in for a hug.

"Come on, let's go to our Scotland."

Chapter 10 And Time

Life on board ship isn't all that different from being on the farm I think, except there are more people to get to know. I choose a few pieces of laundry to take topside to the community washtub and ask Briana to come with me, but she rarely does and it's no different today, so I leave her behind in our small quarters.

Since leaving a month ago, our family has established its own schedule for washing, bathing and eating meals. I've made friends quickly with two young women who are traveling with their parents to Great Britain and through them, I've learned much about their country and what to expect.

It's exhilarating to stand on such a large ship and feel the rise and fall of the ocean under my feet and I carefully step up the ladder to the deck. How could I know I would love it so much?

My skin has begun to freckle from too much time in the sun watching the sea's residents.

The whales are fascinating when they surface and blow out their powerful spouts then play and chase each other. I adore the dolphins who chase along the bow of the ship for miles and at times jump and squeal as they float through the air.

Even the gulls, pelicans and terns who come out of nowhere to soar over our sails are beautiful until they disappear again, leaving me to wonder what land they will be in tomorrow.

❧

Not long after Kenna leaves, I look up to see Dad standing in the doorway.

"Briana, come with me for a walk."

"I don't really feel like it, why don't you go on without me."

He enters the cabin and sits down beside me. "Because I think you need to get out of this room and get some exercise, so get your shoes on and let's go."

We climb the ladder topside and make our way across deck. Kenna waves as she talks to some of the other passengers who wait their turn at the washtub. At the forward rail the wind tangles my hair and blows our jackets open until we grab and button them securely. The sky is full of light clouds and the sun is just heading toward the western horizon.

"What's going through your mind my daughter?" Dad asks, "You've been very quiet the last few days."

"I guess I'm just wondering what life will be like when we get off this ship."

"What would you like it to be?"

"I can't imagine anything but our life back in New Zealand. I keep waiting for some grand thoughts to come to mind, but I guess I'm just not very imaginative."

"Briana, it's alright to use our previous life as a ruler of sorts; we were happy and once we're settled in Aberdeen you'll feel better, I promise. Meanwhile, you need to learn how to fill your time, otherwise you'll be getting cabin-fever."

"I know Dad, I'll try, I promise."

I know well my Briana doesn't adjust as easily to new situations as her sister does. It's good to stand here and talk about the journey and I make a mental note to do this more often until she reconciles herself to her new surroundings and pulls out of her blues.

"You've always been able to capture the beauty of simple things in your drawings, have you done any sketching on the ship?"

"No, it's hard to steady my hand as the ship rolls." She answers me half-heartedly.

233

"Perhaps you need to learn more about where we're going, so you can imagine yourself there." I withdraw a small book from my pocket.

"Here, I borrowed this from the Captain's library for you." She reads the title.

"Scotland, Land of our Fathers". I'll read it today."

"Now take care of it or we'll have to indenture you to the ship until you pay for it." When she looks at me in surprise, I renege, "Oh don't look so worried, I'm only joking. The Captain keeps a library for the crew and I thought this might help you see where you're headed."

"It's very thoughtful of you, really. I've been getting a little bored and maybe reading will make the time pass more quickly."

My children are so different, I think to myself. Kenna, always ready for an adventure; Briana, quiet and reserved, slow to temper; and Angus, my go-to child, always wanting more responsibility and moving forward.

Unknown to Angus, I put in a good word for him with the Captain shortly after we sailed from Port Chalmers. I mentioned his excellent work habits and quality of studies in school during idle conversation, so it was no surprise when Angus burst into our quarters one morning.

"The Captain asked me to be his clerk assistant."

"Wonderful, are you excited?"

"I am, but what if I make a mistake?"

"You do what you know is right, admit it to the Captain, apologize and think of a way to make it up. Things are no different here than back home, except you have a lot more people affected by your mistakes here. I have confidence you'll be a good assistant, but if you don't think you can do it, politely turn him down." He suddenly decides.

"I think I'll accept his offer."

He now spends his days shadowing the Captain, who is pleased with his abilities and uses him to assist with his writing duties. Angus also helps during inventory of the ship's supplies with the First Officer.

Never a lack of inactivity for me since the success or failure of this move depends greatly on good management. Notes and charted business plans for the new granite quarry are always at hand and weekly family meetings are scheduled so my young charges keep up to date in our plans.

"I've written some subjects down I need your input on," I tell them, "the first is finding a place to live. Let's talk about it, I'm interested in anything you have to say or question in regard.

"We'll be staying in hotels until we reach Aberdeen, then I'll find an apartment large enough for us all to have a room of our own. What do you think?"

"Could we spend time in London, Dad, before we travel to Aberdeen, just a few days?" Kenna asks.

"I guess we could, why the sudden interest?"

"You've met Susan and her sister Mary here on board; they live in the London area and their parents have offered to show us the town and shopping if we stay a few days. Please, can we stay a little?"

"What about it? Angus, Briana, would you like to stay for a few days?" Everyone agrees it would be fun and I feel they deserve it after the confinements of the voyage.

"Very well, four days only." I say amid the joy of my girls who are fairly bouncing up and down.

Angus is smiling as well, "Can we look at some of the buildings done in granite Dad? I understand many were built with silver granite."

"How did you find out about that?"

"It came up in conversation with the Captain after hearing our destination is Aberdeen. He said he spent time in the port on many an occasion and is familiar with the granite shipped to London from Aberdeen quarries."

"Hmm, maybe I'll talk with him and find out more about the current shipping industry. It's been years and there's bound to be some changes. Yes, we'll take the building tour and see all that beautiful granite."

The days pass quickly and we experience good weather on the whole with occasional rain storms which give us fresh drinking water.

We stop for provisions before crossing the equator and are thankful that no serious illness has broken out on board beyond the common cold.

To my relief, Briana has finally adjusted to life aboard ship and is now friends with Susan and Mary as well, which helps her pass the time in a better frame of mind.

❧

This early foggy morning in November, my children and I stand at the rail as the ship slides smoothly and quietly through the dark water of the Thames river to a berth in London.

The captain assigned an out-of-the-way spot to us at my request, where we can watch the ship's progress down the river. I watch the children's first reactions to

237

the buildings along the banks and see they are totally into it already, barely noticing I'm here.

Briana sights a grand country estate sitting quite a way back from the river and calls out in case the others haven't seen, pointing to its shrouded beauty in the lifting fog. The estate has a huge lawn leading up to a multi-storied house and she is spell-bound by it.

Kenna watches all the different boats make their way to London and one in particular catches her interest.

"Dad, do you see this little boat loaded with people? They're sitting under a canvas roof."

"They're passengers like us, going to London on business or to visit, maybe even to stay; and some may be from those ships docked over there." I point to the port of Gravesend on the south shore. The little tilt boat moves swiftly on ahead of us, its sails filled by the light breeze.

Fishing boats pass us at the mouth of the river heading out to the North Sea. Crews are busy on their decks readying nets and traps, but a few return friendly waves to Angus, Kenna and Briana.

Upon arrival at our port, huge lines are dropped from the ship to the wharfmen and they proceed to pull the ship closer and tie her off securely.

The Harbor Master comes aboard to talk with the Captain and examine the ship's manifest. Passengers are accounted for as citizens, noncitizens and immigrants. I have my emmigration papers from Scotland and carry them as advised before leaving.

Because I was born in Scotland, I have dual citizenship and can travel freely between New Zealand and the United Kingdom. The children enjoy the same privilege and I carry their christening papers as proof of their place of birth.

The crew begins unloading passenger trunks and we are soon cleared to leave the ship.

'No goat carts this time' I think with a smile as I guide my family down the plank and tell them to stay close and watch their belongings. A man for hire approaches us, asking if we need a cab and where we might be heading.

"Yes, we'll need a cab for four, to the Langham please."

"Aye Sir." He quickly leaves to acquire a cabbie.

"Dad, does the river always smell like this?" Angus asks, wrinkling his nose, "It's terrible."

"I don't remember it this way son, but the years and influx of people have obviously taken their toll. We'll soon be away from here."

The man returns to load our trunks to a dolly and calls us to follow him. He loads and ties them to the top of the carriage, adding the last onto the back. I pay the man's fee, nod to the driver and load up my children then with a tap on the roof, we are off.

The girls look at the well-worn carriage interior as if it's a fairy cart. Angus tries not to look impressed, but I can tell he is.

"It's been many years since I saw the city." I tell them and think of Father when he took me on my first carriage ride.

I anticipate an enjoyable few days as I accompany Kenna and her young friends and tour with Angus. I must make arrangements for transportation to Aberdeen, perhaps a train ride for my brood's enjoyment.

Town traffic picks up as vendors begin to make their rounds with their various wheeled carts and baskets to the large homes on the outskirts of London. Their wares include fresh vegetables, flowers, lamp oil, coal, almost anything a household could require.

School children already walk in uniforms to the local academies with their governesses and businessmen walk briskly up the sidewalks to catch their streetcars. Carriages and cabs are heavy in the business districts as our cab pulls up to the Hotel's front entry at last.

The Langham was newly opened three years prior and featured in the London News back home. My children stare out the windows in awe as a uniformed footman steps to the curb to open the door and helps my young ladies down. The cabman paid, I lead them up the front steps into the massive lobby as our trunks are unloaded and brought behind us.

"Everything is lined with marble." Angus says as he tries to be nonchalant about it all.

"Look at those beautiful chandeliers." Briana comes to a complete stop to gaze upward at the sparkling crystal.

"Good day sir, how may we assist you?" the desk manager asks.

"A suite for the next four days please, I assume you have one with three bedrooms?"

The attendant blanches a bit at the appearance of our family, obviously we're not from London and slightly ship-worn.

"We've just docked from our New Zealand voyage; disembarked at West India wharfs this morning. We're ready to readjust to living on land and what better place to do it than at the Langham?"

The flattery works and the gentleman asks for my signature and names of the children in the large, leatherbound register on the counter.

"We have a suite on the seventh floor sir, with three separate bedrooms. There is a deposit of L1000s for the week; shall I call the bellman to take your bags up?"

"Yes, please." The attendant smiles for the first time since our arrival.

"Thank-you sir, please follow the bellcap with your luggage to the room lift. We hope you enjoy your stay with us, if you require assistance, please use the room service bell in your suite."

We follow the bellcap into a large room-like cage at the end of the lobby. He pulls the doors closed and pushes a lever to the right. The room begins to move and lifts us up off the lobby floor.

"Dad." Briana says in alarm and grabs my arm.

"It's alright" Kenna says, "I read about this, it's called a 'lift' and will take us all the way up the building to our room. Isn't it great?" she beams, thoroughly enjoying herself.

Angus, in contrast to Kenna, stands solidly in the corner not saying a thing until we arrive at with a lurch. The porters let us exit first then wheel the trunks down the hall behind us. Angus' face relaxes now that he's out of the lift.

We step through a lovely french door with Kenna who is first to say "Oh, my!"

The room is decorated with burgundy and cream carpeting in a vine and rose pattern. The silk wallcovering is pale green with pinstripes in a lighter burgundy and a darker green to match the drapes. Large couches and chairs are arranged in the middle of the room and light streams from the high arched windows into the salon. I tip the porter and wait for the door to close behind him.

"Well, what do you think?" I ask them.

"Dad, this is too much." Angus says as he motions around the room. "We can't afford this; L1000s for less than a week?"

"Angus, it's time you realise we can afford this; well, once in a while anyway. Besides, this is a vacation of sorts for all of us and probably the last for a while. You and the girls will be going to university and I'll be building a new business in Aberdeen. We need this, so no more concern over the cost, agreed?"

"You don't have to coax us Dad, we love it." Kenna says as apparently she and Briana are already convinced and both wander off to see which rooms they want.

I sit heavily in one of the big settees, barely settled when I hear Angus call me.

"What is it?" I ask and go to investigate. I find all three in one room taking turns opening and shutting the water taps at the sink and amazed at the hot water in one. Kenna is already eyeing the large marble bath tub at the back of the room and Briana is trying to figure out why a porcelain bowl with a lid is on the other wall.

"We've never had running water, but this is what you can expect ladies and gentleman." And I reach to push the lever down on the 'porcelain bowl" demonstrating the art of flushing. "No outhouses here." I say with a smile.

Their faces remain blank for a few seconds before it slowly dawns on them. Angus starts to snort at the girls and they begin to giggle. I hear their commotion echo from the marble-lined room as I walk back to the salon and ring room service for some lunch.

The next day, we take a walk through Regent's Park then do some shopping. Kenna and Briana each pick out new day dresses and shoes, overcoats for cool days and of course, umbrellas for us all.

We pass a hat shop and I insist they each pick a hat suitable for citywear. With the addition of some personal items I feel my 'little Roses' immediate needs are suitably met.

Angus is another matter and doesn't see shopping for new clothes as anything affecting him. I have to use my Father role to escort him into a large store named Harrods. Luckily, we find a new suit off the rack which doesn't require alteration, an overcoat, then two pair of shoes, three new shirtwaists, two ties, underwear and socks, with a final visit to the instore barber for a trim.

"I'm exhausted" Briana declares. "Can we please sit down somewhere for a fizzie or something?"

"Good idea, how about that place over there?" The sidewalk café is just across the street; weather has cleared and the sun is starting to warm us.

We order fizzies, chocolate for the girls; grape for Angus and I.

"Dad, don't forget, tomorrow we meet Mary and Susan Fenton with their parents."

"Kenna, how can I forget? You've reminded me twice in two hours. Am I giving the appearance of senility?"

"No Dad, I'm just excited to see them and more of the city while we're here, that's all."

"It'll be a great outing and I'm looking forward to getting acquainted with them. You can both wear your new dresses."

The next morning everyone wakes early. We take breakfast in the room then ready ourselves to meet Lloyd and Emily Fenton at ten in the downstairs lobby. They sent a message last evening they will pick us up in their private carriage. Suits me very well as I am ready to be escorted rather than to be the escorter. Yesterday's schedule left me wanting a day of rest and I intend to fit it in as much as possible.

Lloyd proves to be my idea of the perfect man; raised on a farm in upper Manchester, he attended university majoring in agriculture, inherited his father's farm and added additional acreage of his own over the years.

His oldest son manages for him now, leaving him free to travel with his wife Emily and the girls. He's been hybriding sheep for several years to withstand climate change and used this latest visit in New Zealand to close a large sales contract.

The girls seem to enjoy the adventure of new places but Emily, a self-confessed home-body, declares she is very glad to arrive back in Britain 'where I belong.'

We parted with them earlier this evening after a wonderful dinner in the hotel's dining room and count them as our first friends in the U.K. I left them with an open invitation to Aberdeen after we settle in.

From the balcony of our suite, the busy street below soon quiets to a few late arrivals from the train station and I hear a long and lonely wail in the distance as a train engineer makes ready to move down the track.

Thinking of the many people I've met in the last twenty-two years in New Zealand, I try to think of those I left in Scotland before, but it's difficult to see their faces in my mind. Both Rose's and my parents are gone and I have no idea if any of my cousins are still around. Our friends in New Zealand mean the most to me now and I hope they'll be able to visit Aberdeen someday.

"Dad, what are you doing out here?" Angus joins me at the railing to look out over the city.

"Just thinking about our friends in New Zealand, hoping they can visit sometime."

"I know what you mean, I miss James. He's really like a big brother to me and used to rescue me from my sisters once in a while." We laugh together.

"Tomorrow, we'll take a trip uptown and see Parliament and maybe stroll by the Palace?"

"Sounds great." Angus responds.

"Any reason the girls can't come along?"

"No, none I can think of, but give me time—just joking Dad. See you in the morning."

"Good night son."

It's rainy this morning but Londoners hurry about their business as if it were dry weather. We leave the hotel and take a cab past the Parliament building, stopping to get a better look at its architecture. Everyone is astonished at its sheer size and the decorative detail of spire and statuary.

We hear Big Ben ring at noon, his deep voice so memorable it strikes our very souls.

We stop at a small tea shop for sandwiches and hot tea to warm us from the dampness then it's on to the Queen's Palace with its beautiful porticos and fountain. The Beefeaters execute the changing of the guard ceremony; quite impressive. The girls attempt to make one of the gate guards smile by standing in front of him for a few minutes, but true to his orders, he doesn't move or register what he really thinks; *two beautiful young women are in front of me.*

❧

On Thursday I leave Briana with Dad in the salon and go to pack some of my things into my travel trunk brought to the room earlier.

"I'll be right there Kenna." Bri calls after me.

I finish putting neat stacks to pack on the bed, but keep my new travel outfit hanging for the next day's train ride to Aberdeen.

"How long do you think the trip will take?" Briana asks from the doorway.

"Dad said about twelve hours. We have a sleeper so we can get some rest on the way into Edinburgh at least. I believe we have to transfer a couple of times on the way to Aberdeen. You all packed?"

"Most of it, all except toiletries and what I'm wearing on the train." Briana adds.

"Cheer up, we'll make Aberdeen soon enough and get settled in a hotel until we find an apartment." I assure her.

"I miss the farm you know," she continues, "all that open country and gentle sunsets. I never thought I would, but I do. Grand as this has been, I long for its peaceful afternoons. Perhaps I'm not meant to be a city woman." She goes to stand in front of the large window in our room.

"I miss the farm, too. Dad said all his memories of Mother are there and though I only remember bits of her, a feeling of her remains, just knowing it's where she lived." I go to Bri and wrap her in a hug. "We have so few memories of her; we were young, you know?"

"Yes, you're right. But she should be with us, could have been with us..." She couldn't say more for the lump in her throat.

"She can't because it wasn't meant to be and nothing we do can change it. We keep her inside and further her memory; Dad saw to it by funding the Church wing in her name and Catherine's. I think she would love that."

"She would, wouldn't she." Bri agrees.

"Now cheer up. Let's go give Angus a hard time about packing." We laugh as we head toward his room. He really is our favorite brother but he is so much fun to tease.

❧❧

I have our supper brought up to the salon, a last night's treat in London and we sit down to it. "Let's say grace everyone" I prompt as my noisy bunch finally quiets down.

"Dear Lord we thank you for keeping us safe thus far in our travels. Tomorrow we head north and back to my home. Please bless our journey and help as you see fit to get us settled once more. Bless this food and make us truly grateful. Amen."

This morning we take our last thrilling ride down the lift to the lobby. Even Angus says he's grown somewhat accustomed to his stomach lurching as the room starts its descent, but I am positive he will not miss riding in the device at all.

We arrive at King's Cross Station and our trunks are loaded to a baggage cart by an eager porter who follows us into the building to the ticket windows.

"Four tickets to Aberdeen please, first class." I speak through the grilled window to the clerk, who explains we will change trains in Edinburgh to continue on to Aberdeen. The time between London and Edinburgh is approximately ten and a half hours with a thirty minute stop at York for lunch.

"Thank-you very much, what time will the train begin boarding?"

"Forty-five minutes until the train is available for boarding, sir. Your trunks are secured to be loaded then."

"Let's take a look around, shall we?" I note my children are gawking at the high ironwork which holds glass paneled skylights over the entire station floor.

We buy postcards to send to Thomas, Ethan and George and I'm persuaded to buy each a cherry-flavored ice. I also purchase several sandwiches, apples, grapes and bottled drinks to take with since we have only one stop before Edinburgh.

We hear the station master announce the train and walk to the track to find our car. I lift the latch for the girls and Angus follows us in, closing the door firmly behind him. The dark wood-panelled compartment has seats on either side upholstered in red velvet. An oil lamp mounted at the entry from the sidehall will allow us to read or play cards during the trip and two pull-down cots make the car ready for all of us to get some sleep later.

"Tickets please." The conductor enters and quickly clips the London mark on our tickets.

"Welcome aboard." He tips his cap to the girls, "How far are you going today?"

"All the way to Aberdeen." I reply.

"Approximately fifteen hours sir, give or take. We have a thirty minute stop in York and then on to Edinburgh where you'll change to another train for Dundee and Aberdeen. The privy is just down this hall," he motions first to his right, then to his left "drinking water vat at the end here."

In five minutes we hear him call "all aboard" and the train's bell rings. Our car lurches as it joins those in front and we move slowly out of the station, pulled by the puffing, steam-powered locomotive.

"Dad, this is exciting. How fast will we go?" Kenna asks.

"Will the ride be smoother after we build up speed?" Briana asks, already slightly woozy from the swaying of the car.

"How much weight do you think this train can pull, Dad?" Angus asks, thinking of granite as he frequently does of late.

"I think these are all questions you should ask the conductor the next time he stops by; I'll bet he has all the answers because I certainly don't." I love that my intelligent children inquire about such things.

☙♺

I still watch the farms pass by after they all nap; Dad, his head leaning into the corner of his seat; Briana and Kenna on the other bench.

We spent the first hour watching the passing houses until the train left London. Then the countryside began to weave a fascinating scene and it's hard to take my eyes off it. Even the occasional overpass gives one the chance to admire the leaf colors of gold and red scattered on either side of the tracks.

I look at my sisters and Dad, smiling to see them thus. It's rather comforting, this train ride; sort of like being rocked in a cradle. I focus on the future and imagine what it will be like in Aberdeen; what universities we can choose from and where we'll live.

It's all too unimaginable at this point I conclude and give in to easing down in my seat. With arms crossed comfortably over my chest, I join the others in a needed nap.

❦

The train slows and we all wake at the same time slightly disoriented.

"Dad?"

"We must be near York." I say and sit up to stretch my arms over my head. "I could do with a walk-about."

At the York station the conductor announces a thirty minute stop and warns the train will leave on schedule with no waiting for tardy travelers. We decide to take advantage and see what little of the nearby town we can.

We walk briskly down the platform of the old station as we look at the gently sloped green land beyond. It appears the oldest parts of the city are across a river surrounded by an ancient city wall and we can just see the tops of historic buildings and church spires peeking over it.

"Wish we had time to spend, it looks quite intriguing doesn't it?" I remark.

"Oh Dad. Here's a chocolate shop, can we go in." Briana's eyes are on the front window's assortment of crafted chocolates; miniature boxes hold various shapes and sizes of the delectable stuff with hand-painted designs.

"We have time if we don't spend more than five minutes – Angus, time us will you please?" I hold the door open for them; trust Briana to spot food first before history.

Inside we see many choices, jellies and chocolates all packaged and displayed in appealing ways.

"Ok ladies, Angus says we're down to three minutes, make your choices." I announce and select a bag of chocolate cookie crisps for myself.

We walk briskly back to the station and arrive just in time to board our car and drop into our seats before the conductor signals the engineer.

"Remind me not to do this again in a thirty minute stopover," I declare the lesson learned, "and how about some real food before you launch into those chocolates." I pass their sandwiches around with a piece of fruit for each and we picnic together while the countryside moves swiftly by.

Later, we play word games until we notice it's dark outside. The porter arrives to lower the foldup cots over our seats and distributes blankets and pillows.

I sit writing in my journal as Briana and Kenna drift off to sleep across their seats. Angus has already climbed up to one of the cots. Our sleep will be interrupted at Edinburgh, but they are wise to get what rest they can.

The rocking of the train proves to be an excellent sleep aid and the conductor wakes us twenty minutes prior to the station, saying "Twenty minutes to Edinburgh—Twenty minutes to Edinburgh."

The girls stand up to straighten their skirts; obviously concerned with their hair, they make repairs as needed, using the darkness of the window as a mirror to see their reflections.

The Edinburgh station appears as the train pulls to a stop. We collect our parcels and step off to the platform.

I'm concerned about our trunks and go to the baggage car to check on them while Angus and the girls walk to a bench to wait for me. The trunks are soon unloaded and placed up against the wall of the station.

I assign Angus to stand watch while the girls and I go inside to inquire about our next train.

At the ticket window, a white-haired gentleman wearing reading glasses on the end of his nose responds with "She'll be here in about an hour, a little off schedule but here soon enough. Goes into Dundee in about four hours and another four hours to Aberdeen, putting you in around six in the morning."

He hands me back our tickets and instructs, "Make yourselves comfortable, benches are kind of hard, but it's warm in here at least." Smiling, he offers tea but understands it is late and keeps the invitation open, should we change our minds.

I call Angus in from his vigil since the trunks are within my view and the stationmaster's. The girls can apparently sleep under any conditions and have already settled down on their benches while Angus and I sit looking out at the evening light.

"I'm just ready to finally get there." Angus says.

"I know what you mean, I'm ready to sleep for ten hours at our next hotel. London was enjoyable, but not very restful with all the shopping and sightseeing."

"Dad, do you think I could be your intern when you start your quarry business?"

"What makes you think you want to get into the granite business son?"

"I read some newspaper articles in London, about the price of granite, how it's used, how much it's in demand and it seems like most new construction calls for it. Did you know they ship all over the world? I think if a man is smart, he can make a pretty good living at it, especially if he owns the company and his employees are safe and happy."

"I believe it, but I'm surprised you've discovered all this in a few days. I thought you'd want a farm somewhere as much as you seemed to enjoy ours in New Zealand."

"I've changed my mind and I'd like to be involved in the company. It'll give me the experience I need in business and I can still go to university for a degree, as long as I can be flexible enough in my hours with you."

"It's a deal son." We shake on it and it's good to see him growing into a man. I have a positive feeling about Angus.

Chapter 11 Family

The sun is up by the time the train pulls into Aberdeen station and we've managed to capture some additional sleep since the Dundee stop. My children and I rally on the platform for the final leg of the journey, that of transporting ourselves and baggage to a local hotel or inn. Surprisingly, in spite of the early hour, an older gentleman waits by the station entrance and approaches me.

"Take you to your destination Sir?" He asks, touching his cap.

I pull him aside, "Not having been in the city for twenty-two years, I've lost track of accomodations available, can you make some suggestions?"

"My name is Joshua McCabe" the man says, extending his hand to me.

"Daniel Smith, a pleasure to meet you."

"Any Scot who comes home after all this time deserves a handshake." he declares good-naturedly. "What exactly are you looking for?"

"As you can see, we'll need sleeping and living accomodations for four, comfortable, with privacy, clean and warm. I'll be looking for more permanent arrangements, but for now we just need a lodge close to the main streets of the City until we get our bearings; in the range of say, £10s a week."

"A very suitable lodge off Holburn below Union might be the ticket sir;" Mr McCable replies, "not the center of town but a brisk walk will bring you to the banking district and stores. In view of your young family, I believe it would be most suitable; I know the widow Gordon who owns the Lodge and she has two children as well. Would you like to take a look?"

"Given our present situation, I think it's a very good idea Mr. McCabe."

"Call me Josh, most do." He begins to load the trunks to his wagon which is nearby.

The ride to the Lodge takes less than thirty minutes and we ride paved streets all the way, a novelty for all of us. I sit by Josh in front and Angus, Briana and Kenna sit on the bench behind us. We pass many splendid homes on the way as well as a cemetery and a public garden kept by the city.

Josh pulls his team to a stop in front of the Hawthorne Lodge. It appears to be a large mansion, perhaps as many as fifteen to twenty rooms with a wing on either side of a silver granite entry. The entry door appears to have been part of a portico for coaches at one time before the street was widened and the drive-thru eliminated.

We climb down from our seats and approach the large door, using the bell to summon the proprietor.

I'm surprised when a woman of my age opens the door.

"Good morning, may I help you?" she asks pleasantly.

"Yes, good morning. I apologize for the earliness of the hour, but we've just arrived on the train from London and my family and I are in need of several rooms."

"I see. Well, you've had quite the morning already haven't you? Come in, all of you," she motions to us and to Josh as well.

"We've had early callers off the train in the past, so please feel at ease." She says. "Would you like a cup of tea or coffee after your long journey?"

"If it isn't too much trouble, it sounds wonderful." The children answer as well with "Yes, please."

"Good. Come through to the parlor, I've just had a fire laid and it's taking the morning chill off." She takes us the few steps into a large, bright room off the wide hallway.

"Forgive me, I'm Philomena Gordon." She extends her hand to me and I introduce the children.

"So nice to meet all of you, sit down and warm yourselves. You come at an opportune time as I've just had several weekly guests leave for London. Allow me to explain the living arrangements here at the Lodge." After using a bell pull near the fireplace, she sits across from us, straightening the skirt of her blue wool day dress.

"As you can see, this is not your usual lodge setting, it's my home, left to me by my husband who passed away five years ago. I have two children, who may be the age of your children, both are seventeen, twins you see."

"My sister and I are twins as well." Kenna speaks up.

"You should all get along splendidly then; their names are Patrick and Amanda." A woman comes to the doorway.

"This is our housekeeper Anna. Would you please bring a tea tray for our guests and put some sweets on it as well, I imagine they're quite hungry after their long trip."

"Of course mam." Anna replies and turns away down the hall.

"When my husband passed," Mrs. Gordon continues, "I decided to let our rooms, not only to keep the Estate going but to add some purpose to my life. So we have fourteen sleeping rooms upstairs; the hallway running through the north and south wings offers two designated bathing and toilet rooms on either wing, one for ladies and one for gentlemen.

"Guests have full use of the living areas downstairs and the kitchen. Meals are served by Anna for breakfast and dinner in the diningroom and included in the weekly sum. I make the guests responsible for their own lunch as it is hard to predict just how many will be in for lunch or out, I'm sure you understand?"

"Perfectly. We will require four separate rooms, on the same hallway if possible, but I would like to see the rooms first, if you don't mind."

"Of course, why don't we just go up now and when we return, your tray should be ready and we can sit and enjoy it. Josh, please stay for a cup as well if you can?" she invites.

"Thank-you mum, I'll just check in with Anna in the kitchen and be back here when you return."

We walk out to the grand staircase in the entry and ascend to the second floor. A crystal chandelier hangs centered over the entry hall and I note there are two more levels above us.

Mrs Gordon turns to the right in the north hallway which is beautifully carpeted in an oriental pattern. She opens the first door on the left and steps back to let us enter.

It's a larger room than expected and two windows are flooding early morning light over the furnishings of the victorian-style room. A high bed sits to the right with bedstands at each side and gaslights mounted over them on the wall.

A fireplace, laid and ready to light, is opposite and two arm chairs sit in front to either side. A small desk with ample room to do correspondence upon is placed under one window and the room's heavy drapes on both windows will surely keep it draft-free. An adequate armoir for storing the resident's clothing sits just inside the door to the left.

"I am quite surprised at the size Mrs Gordon, it may be the girls could easily share a room, but we'll discuss it downstairs after they have time to consider it."

"Very well Mr. Smith, now let's look at the other three rooms and you may choose which you prefer."

Mrs Gordon points out the two bathing and toilet rooms on the hallway, which are obviously very clean. I note both have running water, a plus in a house of this age.

"I've been able to upgrade our plumbing to the modern age Mr. Smith," she says proudly, "and I've had no complaints from my residents."

Back downstairs in the parlor, Anna has placed a large tray with tea service and another with an assortment of cinnamon buns warm from the oven along with a pot of butter.

Josh sits on a side chair finishing off his cup. "Anna gave me a cup ahead Mrs Gordon so I can return to work, hope you don't mind?"

"Not at all Josh, I certainly understand, please don't feel obligated to socialize when you have duties that call."

"Well girls, have you decided to share or have separate rooms?" I ask.

Kenna looks at Briana who nods her agreement, "Plenty of room for us to share, Dad."

"Angus, I assume you would rather have your own space and not have to put up with my late night journal habits?"

"If it's alright Dad...then yes."

"There you have it Mrs Gordon, three rooms it is, now it's just the matter of the deposit and fees."

"Excellent. I asked Anna to prepare a bill for you, one week in advance of course, which will be refunded with proper notice of intent to vacate within one week.

"Yes, this looks satisfactory." I take out the necessary monies and hand them to her.

"Josh, I can help you unload those trunks now; looks like this is our new residence in town for at least two weeks."

"Aye sir, I'll just drive the rig around back and meet you there." He quickly leaves by the front door.

The trunks are brought up first to our respective rooms and stacked against the walls until we decide what we need for our stay. Later they'll be stored in the attic.

Within a few hours though, the children and even I, put off the bulk of the unpacking to lay our travel-worn selves into our feather beds, sleeping soundly right through dinner.

అుఖా

I open my eyes to the sun peeking through an opening in the drapes and sit up to look around. I wonder if the rest of the family is awake since we've obviously missed the past twelve hours in sleep.

My trunks are stacked against the wall, untouched from yesterday; fewer than my sisters' certainly, but more than I want to deal with right now. Nothing for it though; I need clean clothes and toiletries. I crawl off the high bed to find a pair of trousers in the first trunk and open another for one of the new shirts Dad helped me purchase in London. I add a corduroy jacket, clean socks and underwear. A hot bath is what I need now I think and take everything with me to the bathing room.

Halfway there a door on the right opens and I'm surprised when a red-haired girl about my age comes into the hall. She's startled at the sight of me and stops suddenly. At that point, it's painfully obvious to me I'm still in my nightshirt and slippers, hair mussed and sticking up.

She looks down and away from me then says "Good morning" and quickly continues down the hall to the stairs.

"Good morning" I reply over my shoulder and roll my eyes upward at my appearance. I open the bathing room door but turn around to glance back at her. Seeing her glance at me too, I quickly close the door and in the process drop everything, including my comb and razor which clatter noisily across the tiles.

"Good grief." I lean against the door for a few seconds to collect myself. *She is very pretty.*

❦

Kenna and I awake early enough to take turns soaking in the tub of the Ladies bathing room.

"Heaven." I declare as I hand off the soap and tooth powder to Kenna for her turn. By breakfast, we are both ravenous before Dad and Angus appear, so we decide to go downstairs to the dining room together.

We're surprised to see several guests at the table already and hear some voices in the parlor as well.

"Come in, come in, help yourselves at the buffet, plenty to choose from." Anna invites us.

We walk to a massive huntsman credenza on the far wall to pick up plates from a stack. The breakfast choices are almost as numerous as the many types of game depicted on the wooden table's design; Deer, pheasant, rabbits, and ducks as well as partridge and grouse are carved in relief on the heavy wood surround and the table itself looks a full eight foot length, centered as it is on the room's end wall.

There are thick slices of ham, both pork sausage and black, eggs hard and soft with fresh tomatoes sliced and broiled cheese on top and a finnan haddie, a beautiful smoked haddock steak poached in cream, keeps warm in its heavy china server. A porridge pot holds its traditional breakfast with currants mixed in for good measure.

Carafes of tea and coffee sit at the opposite end of the table with some sort of buttery croisants or rolls on a plate nearby. Fresh strawberries, red raspberries with whipped cream and their counterparts in jam pots, complete the board.

Kenna and I help ourselves then look for a place to sit together. The guests are friendly and introduce themselves to us, including where they're from. We are the only ones from New Zealand, though Anna says they've had one or two visitors in the past.

"Our father Daniel was born and raised right here in Aberdeen and has come home to start a new business." Kenna offers.

"Oh, what does he do?" a Mr. McCowry asks.

"He, rather we, raised sheep in New Zealand."

"But I believe he intends to go into the granite business here." I finish for her.

"Ah, does he now?" the man smiles. "Would he have a quarry in his sights then?"

"Not yet, but soon." Dad answers from the diningroom doorway. Taking in the room at a glance, he crosses to us to plant a kiss on our heads. "Good morning girls."

"Good morning Dad."

Angus soon appears, fresh-scrubbed and looking quite handsome, enhanced by the fact he's wearing clean clothes for the first time in two days. Feeling like a new man, he piles a plate high with a taste of near everything on the sideboard.

"My, my. We'll have to raise our provisions list for this one." Anna jokes but sees Angus' alarm.

"Oh, now don't mind me sir, I like to tease the young people a bit. Raised two of me own bairns and know the appetite of a growing lad well." She offers to get his coffee and brings it to the table.

"Good morning all, how are we today?" Mrs. Gordon enters and takes her seat at the head of the table. "I see our newest guests are with us this morning; has everyone been introduced?"

Mr. McCowry makes a point of answering first, "Yes, we have, thank-ye mam. Mr. Smith is looking to join the quarry industry in Aberdeen." He says it, proud he already knows something about us. "Why don't you tell us more about it Mr. Smith?" He asks.

I look at him calmly; "I don't believe I know to whom I'm speaking sir, what brings you to Aberdeen?"

"I'm, ah, here seeking employment in the granite industry, sir." He clears his throat, embarassed I've beaten him at his own game.

"That so, what part of the granite industry?" I fire off before he has a chance to rally.

"I've been a granite layer for ten years, buildings, streets, that sort of thing in London. I decided to come further north to ah...get out of the congestion of the population."

I notice his hands are calloused and his upper body is muscled and strong, supporting his story to some degree. As to why he left London, it's anyone's guess but no reason to be rude to him I decide.

"Perhaps we can get better acquainted at a later time sir?"

"Yessir, name the time." He urges.

"I will." I reply then turn to my family to signify the end of the conversation.

"Everyone sleep well?" I inquire and am happy to hear they did.

"Lovely accomodations Mrs. Gordon." I smile at her as she nods and Mr. McCowry takes his leave.

The rest of the morning is spent unpacking and Mrs Gordon gives me a key so we can have free access to the attic, should we need further from our trunks.

Kenna and I finish putting away our clothing by early afternoon and decide to explore the house and gardens. On the way down the first floor hall, we glance into an oak paneled room and spy stocked library shelves. We both enter to browse but are surprised to see two people our age at the library's table reading over some open books.

"Please excuse us, we didn't know you were here." Kenna says.

"It's quite alright," the girl rises from her chair.

"I'm Amanda Gordon and this is my brother Patrick. You must be the twins my mother mentioned; welcome to our home." She extends her hand to Kenna, then to me.

I notice Patrick doesn't bother to rise and sits observing us. I'm unsure of his thoughts, but it's clear he doesn't intend to greet us.

Never one to take a hint, Kenna says "Hello Patrick, I'm Kenna."

He exhibits a half smile, "Good afternoon Kenna, Briana." Then he returns to his reading.

"We'll just leave you alone so you can continue your studies, we didn't mean to interrupt" I say in apology.

"Please," Amanda says, "it's so nice to see someone our age here. Would you like to come to tea at four?"

"Why yes, that would be lovely." Kenna replies.

We continue our walk to the kitchen entrance at the back of the house and step into a lovely landscaped garden. A raised-bed vegetable garden lays to the right and masses of roses and other late-bloomers are all around the walls. At the garden's center, water from a bubbling fountain forms a duck pond and we sit on a bench to watch two duck go in for a swim.

"He certainly doesn't seem like a very cheerful sort does he." Kenna says, referring to Patrick; more a statement than a question.

"Probably having a bad day, no need to take it personally. Perhaps he'll improve by tea time." I answer and we laugh as we proceed with our walk.

"I like Amanda, I wonder if they're at university yet?" Kenna says.

❧

I finish my unpacking early and decide to walk uptown to the Bank and check on the monies transferred from New Zealand. It's pleasant to get some exercise and to see the changes in the town, which has certainly grown since Rose and I left.

The children should be introduced to their heritage here I think as I walk and make a mental note to schedule free time with them for a family tour. The parish cemetery at Kingswell where all our kin lay should be included and the old farm might be of interest to them, too, if its still there.

Union Street with its familiar greystone buildings, sidewalks and streets is much busier now. People haven't changed in their demeanors though; still courteous in greeting the stranger, but progress and growth have sped up their pace considerably since my youth.

I stop to look into shop windows along the way and am surprised there are so many; a lady's millinery shop which I suppose Mena visits; and a jewelry store as well. A library and reading room are also new to me which I will visit at a later date.

At the Bank of Scotland, I'm happy to find our "nest egg" is growing with the investments Sam Sinclair advised me on. I reregister my contact address in town and make a point of meeting the investments manager to get acquainted. My father taught me early on; 'People are more careful with your money, if they know who you are'. I smile at the unexpected memory of him.

On the way home, I stop in a wine shop and buy two bottles of white for dinner then visit the chemist's shop to browse and introduce myself.

The newstand on the corner renders several periodicals to catch me up on the latest since the isolation of travel, including an issue of the New Zealand Post, a pleasant surprise.

At my final stop, I make an appointment with a gentleman's outfitter for next week. He has an interesting display of trousers, jackets and hats in his window and I realize my existing wardrobe consisting of one out-of-style dress suit won't exactly project a businessman's image here.

It's almost four when I arrive back at Hawthorne and walk directly to the kitchen with the wine. Anna is laying a tea tray with little cakes and the high-ceilinged kitchen makes it a cozy scene with its curtains at two big windows framing the view into the garden.

A small table and chairs sit in its center and large white cabinets surely render plenty of storage. Copper pots, scrubbed to a shine and iron pans of every sort hang from a rack on one wall. Anna looks up in surprise.

"Oh, good afternoon sir, what can I do for you?" she asks, brushing a strand of graying hair back into her kitchen cap and straightening her apron.

"Anna, I just acquired this wine on the way home and thought Mrs. Gordon might like it to serve with dinner, what do you think?"

"I think she'll be thrilled sir. We're having cod tonight and this is perfect."

"Well, it worked out well didn't it." I return her smile.

"Yes it did sir. Anything I can get for you? The young ones are in the parlor having their tea together and I'm just about to bring this tray to them."

"Here let me bring it for you, it looks quite heavy."

"Oh, that's not necessary sir, I can handle it."

"But I insist, you lead the way Anna."

"Very well, thank-you sir."

I follow her to the parlor where Angus and the girls sit with Mrs. Gordon's son and daughter. The latter has the most remarkable red hair all in ringlets. Her brother reminds me of Angus, with his dark hair and eyes.

"Here we are," Anna announces, "courtesy of Mr. Smith, I might say."

"Hello." I approach them and set the tray down on a side table; "I'm Daniel" and Angus introduces Patrick and Amanda.

"Won't you have some tea?" Amanda invites.

"But I don't want to interrupt your party."

"Sir, I would be honored if you'd stay," Patrick speaks up. "My sister and I are dying to hear about New Zealand."

"Very well then. What would you like to know?"

"I hear of natives with tattoos and wild hair, have you seen them?" Amanda asks.

"Saw several often since 1848 and one became my friend over the years."

"Tell us about them sir, we don't get to hear accurate information and the papers tend to exaggerate I think." Patrick says.

So, I tell them all I know about the Maori, the good and the not so good and our experiences over the years. When I finish, they're quiet for a while.

"Do you think they will survive?" Patrick asks.

"A good question. I believe they will, but their lives are changed forever with so many moving to their land. They'll keep their history sacred and alive by continuing to tell their 'whakapapa', their genealogic stories, to new generations."

I didn't realise Mrs. Gordon had been standing by the door listening.

"That was wonderful Mr. Smith. Thank-you for talking to my children and answering their questions. It's certainly a perspective we wouldn't hear in schools this side of the Atlantic."

"Please, call me Daniel and you are very welcome."

"Then, you must call me Mena, it's the name my family and friends use."

"Mena it is." I return her smile.

The next day I walk my family uptown to see the "silver city." It's a rare clear day and the sun shines off the light gray granite of the buildings, making the quartz in them sparkle. I want them to know about our roots and seeing the city today at its best is a perfect introduction.

"It's beautiful." Kenna and Briana touch the rough, cool granite of a building.

"Where does the granite come from?" Briana asks.

"The silver is mined locally and was brought in by teams of work horses. The various colored granites come from all over and their use depends upon the architect's design and what he recommends for color and type. A few come from local suppliers such as the rose-colored granite, but others may come by train or even boat."

I take them next to The Cathedral of St Machar by carriage. We pass through the gatehouse and find ourselves in its green and landscaped cemetery. The stones are granite, some quite ornate.

"Many of the past Bishops are buried here. It's rumored part of William Wallace's remains were interred here in 1305." Our carriage stops in front of the building.

"The church is called a high kirk Presbyterian under the Church of Scotland. The site had Celtic roots but the Normans built a cathedral here in 580 A.D. The cathedral was destroyed over and over by acts of war, fire and natural disasters. But look, it survives today because of generations of believers who rebuilt and restored it."

We walk inside to see the light through beautiful stained glass panels on its west wall and drink in the quiet beauty. My children are silent in the Cathedral's spiritual presence; Kenna places a hand on one of the cool granite walls.

"This is part of your heritage." I say quietly, "You're from a strong, hearty line and our forefathers' blood runs in you. Be strong in life as they were, go after what you want and meet what life brings with God's strength in your life."

"Oh Dad," Kenna says, "if you don't already know it, you're our inspiration and always have been." Briana agrees.

Angus, who is usually too reserved to speak such things, adds "I learn from you Dad and will continue to do so as long as we're together."

I'm speechless as I stand looking at them and for a moment I feel Rose is by my shoulder.

Chapter 12   Liasons

This fall, after much discussion and thought, both Kenna and Angus decide to enter the University of Aberdeen; Angus to pursue a degree in Law; Kenna to attend classes with him, but as a woman she will not receive a degree.

Her professor says she is impressive in her persistance and could be of use to a "real" lawyer in his practice. Little does he realise what he's set in motion, unwittingly providing motivation for her to push forward against all criticism as a career woman in a law office.

Angus believes his studies will give him an edge in the competitive business of granite and looks forward to doing his internship in our company's startup phase to enhance his studies.

Briana, my quiet one, decided to enlarge on her art abilities and entered the School of Science and Art earlier this summer. She admits to her gift of drawing and wants to move further to photography, a growing interest very popular everywhere and she is intrigued.

Her teachers advise the study of art can enhance her abilities as a photographer.

I'm very proud of each one of them and with my young adult family in school and busy with their studies, I find myself mostly alone for the first time in years. It affords me ample time to find my place in life again and pursue the new business.

Exploring land parcels in Aberdeenshire, the surrounding area outside the city, is top priority since nothing of interest is up for sale locally. Angus wants to use his break during the holidays to do so and I gladly hand it over to him.

In the meantime, I find the latest City Directory for 1868-1869 in the parlor and begin reading about the City's craftsmen, commercial businesses, shipping and railroad contacts. I write a scheduling list of those I wish to meet with, including two architects, a sculptor working with granite and several granite finishers who polish and cut to order.

Rather than directly compete with the giant, well-established Rubislaw and Kenmay quarries, I might better establish a smaller, more compact operation catering to specialties of the sculptor and more artistic users for the housing and building markets.

As I run down the stairs this morning for one of my appointments, I fail to see Mena approaching from the back hall and we collide at the entry landing.

"I am so sorry." I exclaim and grab her elbow to keep her steady. "Are you alright?" She's laughing and straightens her hat.

"I'm quite fine Daniel, no need to worry. Where are you off to in such a rush?"

I notice the color of her eyes, a deep brown with gold flecks, matches the color of her hat and wonder why I haven't noticed their color before.

"I'm heading uptown to meet with a granite sculptor. And you, if I may ask?"

"Just out to do a little shopping."

"Well, why don't we walk together?" I ask.

"That would be very nice, I'd love to."

"How are Amanda and Patrick doing in school, Mena? I don't see much of them anymore." I ask as we walk up the sidewalk toward Union Street.

"They're a studious pair. Actually they've been spending evenings in the library with Angus and Kenna, speaking of which, how are they liking the University?" she asks.

"They've really put themselves into their courses. The good part about taking the same course is being able to discuss the day's homework together. I worried about Kenna's choice of such a daunting career but she's weathering the classes very well."

"She's certainly chosen the road not travelled and it's spread to Amanda." Mena remarks.

"Yes, sorry about that. When Kenna told me Amanda followed, I hoped you weren't too put off by it."

"She's picked an arduous route for the times and they both put up with daily petty criticism regarding women in Law, most of it from their fellow classmates. But I know her strength; when she makes up her mind, she will pursue any challenge to success and I know Kenna will, too. Some day in the not so distant future, I look forward to seeing both of them receive recognition and a certificate for their studies."

"I do worry about my quiet Briana though. She has no one to confer with but her instructors."

"Daniel, I wouldn't worry about her. She is very serious about her art and prefers to draw more than anything else, don't you agree?"

"I do, but sometimes it's a problem for her. She's so shy and doesn't seek out people to talk and socialize with." I relate Briana's experience during our voyage to Scotland.

"She's lucky to have you, Daniel. My children miss their father very much and though I try to fill the space, I've never been entirely successful, especially with Patrick."

"I know what you mean. When Rose passed away, it took me several years to find my place as a single parent. I'm afraid I became distant as a father for them at first, especially the girls. It became more the other way around with them pushing me back to normalcy."

"You had that too? Amanda kept finding things to distract me from my grief after the first year. In fact my lodge evolved from an idea of hers to turn our home into a high class boarding house.

"Imagine, my twelve year-old daughter suggesting such a thing. She had no idea of the ramifications of women in business, but it did start me thinking."

"How did you come around to the idea of the Lodge?"

"One day I looked at my life which consisted of busy work around the house and Church on Sunday. Needlework is not a favorite of mine and it seemed to be all there was in life for a woman alone. But I'd reached my limit and thought again of Amanda's idea, only a better version.

"I opened our home as an up-scale lodge, charging enough to ensure the occupants would be of some substance, well educated and mannered. I wanted it be family friendly, a clean and comfortable haven for travelers who didn't want a hotel atmosphere."

"Ever have someone staying who revealed their true colors and became a problem?" I ask.

"One or two; Mr. McCowry, whom you met your first morning at breakfast being one. I had to ask him to leave later that evening."

"Yes, he did seem to be somewhat volatile, though I couldn't put my finger on his exact story."

"A Sheriff's officer came to Hawthorne the next day to inquire about our Mr. McCowry; he left some trouble in London and a warrant out for his arrest, something petty, but nonetheless, we couldn't have him here."

"Ah, I suspected something of the sort. Shame though, I considered offering him a job as he said he worked in the granite industry in London."

"What a shame, but truthfully he probably wouldn't have been an asset to you Daniel."

"You're right, of course. Well here we are, my first appointment. Mena, would you like to have some lunch while we're out?"

"Well, I have two shops to visit, but would enjoy it. I'll be at the hatter just up the street for a little while and at the upholsterer's next to look for some fabric."

"Perfect, I'll find you. This shouldn't take more than thirty minutes."

When I enter Mr. Hegge's studio, I'm amazed at the examples of work displayed. Sculpted columns of granite and marble in various styles stand at the corners of the room. Fireplace mantels and lintels are erected on the studio walls and samples of various marbles and granites are laid on tables for perusal by prospective buyers. A gentleman in suit and tie approaches me.

"Good morning, may I be of assistance?"

"Good morning, yes, I'm here for an early appointment with Mr. Hegge."

"I'll let him know you're here sir."

In a few moments, a burly man in his forties with work apron over his suit, calls out as he walks from the back of the shop.

"Hello. You must be Mr. Smith. Welcome to my studio." he says enthusiastically. "Please come sit down." He leads the way to a meeting area with comfortable chairs and a table.

"Thank-you Mr. Hegge I appreciate your time, I know it's hard to be pulled away from your work."

"It is, but I'm intrigued because you mentioned when you scheduled, you are late of New Zealand. What brings you to Scotland?"

"Well, my wife and I emigrated to New Zealand in 1848. After her death, I decided to return and look at the granite business."

"Ah, well, as you can see it's been flourishing here in Aberdeen. You know our biggest quarries; the Kenmay a few miles down the road, John Fyfe runs it. The Rubislaw opened many years ago and is still going strong, it's quite a large excavation here in town.

"Then Petershead in Bodam which is maintaining; I understand they're waiting for rail access to boost their operation. Lots of competition in the field, I hope you're prepared with experience for it Mr. Smith?"

"My plan is to find a niche industry in granite; one which none of the top three quarries can cost-effectively supply.

"In earlier days, I was an experienced cutter in Rubislaw and left when the economy slowed. I worked on the outside, laying street setts and erecting ornamental work on buildings and in monuments. So, yes, I believe I do know granite well."

"Excuse me for saying so, but even with your experience, it can be a cuthroat business. I wish you well in your endeavor, though."

"I appreciate it Mr. Hegge and value your opinion very much. You've been involved in the industry through the more recent years, so I'll just ask the question; do you believe there's room for another quarry of the type I describe?"

He thinks for a minute and replies, "Room – yes, especially if the new quarry yielded specialty stone such as red, blue, or other rare colors. We have an abundance of silver and gray from the 'top three' as you call them, but specialty granites must be shipped in, adding greatly to the cost of the project."

"Good news, but of course it will depend upon what resources are found. Here's something else I'm curious about; with all the granite yards in the area, how many have exclusive contracts with the big three quarries?"

"I can't answer with any certainty Mr. Smith, contracts are something of a private matter. As you probably know there's no shortage of granite yards in Aberdeen, upwards of twenty or thirty I'd say and each one sells headstones as well as fancy finishes for buildings, parks and homes, as you see here..." he sweeps his arm around the studio.

"It takes a lot of initiative to stay on top, not just business acumen, but creativity, one of the reasons I run my ad internationally and ship by sea to other countries."

I nod in agreement. "I'd like to do business with you in the future sir, as soon as I'm setup; is it something you might consider?"

"I ne'er say nae to a Scotsman, Mr. Smith. If you find something that tweeks my interest in granite and the price is right, this could be the start of a good business relationship. Keep in touch if you need more input, I'd be glad to see what you can do."

After a tour of the shop, we shake hands and I request he keep my visit under his hat until I am ready to announce the business.

I smile as I walk the sidewalk again. I know the quickest way to get news around is to tell someone to keep it under their hat and I plan to make the remark to all those I visit. I estimate by this time next week, I may be contacted by some of the smaller quarries in the area.

Now it's up the street to the hat shop Mena said she'd visit, but upon inquiring, she's left a message to meet her at the Waverly Hotel dining room on Saint Magnus Court. I hail a cab to the hotel off Guild St., one of the older buildings in the city built around the time of the train service startup.

At the hotel's dining room I inquire of the matre'd then see her smile at me from across the room. A pretty smile I think as I work my way through the tables to her side.

"Hello, have you been waiting long?"

"No, I just arrived a few minutes ago. How did your meeting go?"

"Actually quite well, I met with John Hegge, who answered some questions about the granite industry here in Aberdeen."

"Wonderful. If I had know you were seeing John, I would have introduced you. We've been neighbors for a long time, his wife is one of my friends."

"I should have known you two would be acquainted–probably travel in the same social groups?"

"When Phillip was alive, but I've become quite satisfied to let a lot of that go. Let's order, I'm starved and you're probably close to the same."

After a very enjoyable lunch, we ride back to Hawthorne via cab and I come to her aid to carry packages to the foyer table as instructed.

"It was a lovely lunch," Mena says, "and it's so much nicer than eating alone isn't it?"

"Yes, it is. We should do this again."

"I'll hold you to it Mr. Smith." She smiles then turns to her packages and I am soon back upstairs in my room. As I change from my good jacket, I must say no woman has interested me since Rose, until now.

In the coming weeks, I meet several small granite yard owners and their discussions compare favorably with Mr. Hegge's. They tell me speciality granite is in demand, not necessarily something they can get from the 'big three' and usually ordered and shipped from a third location.

So, my next step is to gain an understanding of the local geography and pinpoint what other nearby areas to explore. Ideally, I want options within a certain radius with access to train service and seaports so we can move the granite to buyers in Scotland, England and ultimately other countries.

It's late November, the weather is nippy and winter almost upon us when Angus and I finally sit down to talk about our progress.

"First, how're your studies going son?" I throw another scoop of coal on the fire grate.

"Well I have a new professor who loves what he does and expects everyone else to love it too. We've lost three more students from those I started with."

"That's good though, right? I mean, he gives you more challenges than your other professor did?"

"Yes, it's good, in fact he may have saved me from following the others. I was beginning to get bored." He smiles at me a little oddly.

"What?" I ask.

"What's going on with you Dad, you look...well, healthier or something."

"Do I? I'm back in my homeland, maybe that's it."

"Or maybe it's Mena?" Angus smiles slyly.

"Ok, we'll have no discussions on the dear woman, except to say...maybe it is. Now, moving on..." I say quickly as Angus attempts to ask more, but is stopped.

"I need your help in locating some sites for the quarry and to bring in samples from potential sites in the ten mile radius. We'll need to find a geographical survey of Scotland for the area, perhaps at the Surveyor's office?

"Our other option is to get out in the countryside and talk to some landowners and farmers, to see what they know of their land and what lies underneath it. Can you help me?"

"I've already planned to do so on break for the holidays." Angus replies. "I'll saddle up to canvas some of the surrounding residents. It'll feel good to get out in the open for a change."

"Splendid, I've been hoping you'd say that. Keep a log on who you see and where so I don't revisit them. You're going to need a good mount you can depend upon, so I'm giving you a check for the Bank now..." I pause to write out a check at the desk.

"When you find one you like, put a deposit down, get your tack, saddle, anything you need. You know horses well enough, you don't need my approval, just look your choice over thoroughly and check with Mrs. Gordon on rental of a stall in her barn."

"I will Dad. I should be able to come up with some possibilities for you by January. What about our equipment needs? Have you investigated?"

"Little early for it; equipment is tricky. We can't order until we have the quarry confirmed and purchased. And, it will take a while to get what we need unless we buy used, which I would rather not do."

"Let me investigate the latest equipment, perhaps in Glasgow," Angus suggests. "If we get prices, production and delivery times, at least we'll have all the info together when we need it."

"Good idea son, you appear to be on top of this. We need to start right and that means being prudent with our money but getting the best equipment for our situation so breakdowns don't hold up production and ultimately money flow."

"Agreed and the same goes for hiring experienced granite cutters. I think we need to pay a few cents more per hour to lure men away from the other quarries. I hear some go to America to work seasonally and many never return."

"America eh?" I write a reminder in my notes.

"I believe the Americans will become real competitors. Their resources are phenomenal and only beginning to be discovered on the east coast." Angus adds.

"Good information son, keep you ears open and read everything you can from overseas. Bring it along for our meetings and we'll share what we find."

Briana returns from classes, flushed from the chill wind blowing outside and carrying her artist box with all her brushes, paints and papers,.

"Here you two are." She smiles at me and drops a kiss on my cheek. "I have wonderful news Dad. I've been invited to enter the annual Aberdeen art competition in May."

"Very good news Bri. Do you know what you're going to enter yet?" I ask.

"I've decided to paint a canvas of Hawthorne. It's a beautiful building and part of Aberdeen history; perfect for my entry." She's beaming and the sight does this father good.

♨

The parlor is pleasantly quiet as I read the daily newspapers when the front door suddenly opens and Mena rushes in with her arms full of packages, dropping all on the entryway table.

"Here, let me help." I rush over to the door in time to meet her with a second load.

"What is all this?" I marvel at the sheer number of boxes and bags she's bringing from the cab.

"It's shopping for Christmas. We only have two weeks."

"Oh....yes." I go silent for a moment, "You're right." The cabdriver brings the remaining boxes to the door behind her then deposits his load on the floor beneath the now full table.

"You haven't started yet have you?" she laughs at my expression.

"Well...no."

"Don't worry, still plenty left in the stores, I haven't bought it all." She turns to the driver and sends him on his way with a nice tip.

"Would you like me to move these someplace else for you?" I ask as I survey the mountain before me.

"No, it's quite alright, Anna and Josh will take them up to my room so I can wrap and hide them.

"Amanda and Patrick are terrible – they always find their gifts before Christmas, but I'm going to fool them this year and say they're adults now and they're only getting one gift each."

"Let me know how it works, I have two the same age, remember? That trick didn't work for me last year."

"Oh no, but you can't blame a girl for trying."

She turns to walk back to the kitchen, but I call her back.

"Mena, there's something I need to discuss with you, but never seem to have had the time over the past few weeks; do you have a few minutes now?"

"Certainly, shall we go into the parlor and sit by the fire?"

"We originally planned to stay a couple of weeks upon arrival and yet, here we still are." I tell her.

"Oh no, you're leaving and before Christmas, too. Daniel please think it over and at least stay through the holidays, it's been so nice having you all here."

"Well, I'm glad you feel that way because here's what I'm going to ask; is it acceptable to make a more permanent arrangement?

"My family and I are happy here...our children seem to be enjoying each other's company and we all love Anna who continues to spoil us. In fact, they think you're pretty wonderful as well."

"What about you Daniel?" she asks.

"Well, I think...that is...you're...special, in every way Mena."

She blushes and drops her eyes from mine on the premise of straightening her skirt, so I continue.

"If you have no objections, we'd like to stay on and make this our home for at least the next six months."

"I think it would be just grand Daniel. Truth is, I'm a little tired of the constant turn-over of visitors though I never thought I'd say it. It's been nice to know you all are here when I return home, or when we plan dinner, knowing what everyone likes. It's worked very well and I'm happy you're staying on."

"Thank-you Mena. I'll let the children know, they'll be relieved as they weren't looking forward to moving out. So...better get those presents upstairs before the kids get home, eh?"

"Oh. You're right." She quickly jumps up to call Anna and Josh from the kitchen for the task.

Briana sits in the back garden, bundled up in her overcoat and muffler, her feet on a folded blanket and another blanket over her lap as she sketches the back of our house with its garden and fountain. She hears me approach and turns, startled out of her concentration.

"You are so bad Patrick Gordon; trying to scare the wits out of me." she scolds. I notice her blue eyes are surprisingly blue today in contrast to her cheeks and nose which are pink from the cold.

"What? I'm just walking toward my house, not my fault if you were startled" I tease her and look at the drawing she's begun on the canvas.

"This is really good Bri, how long have you been at it?"

"I just started, it took me longer to get settled in these blankets than it did to draw."

"I really like it." I continue to stare at the details she's captured so perfectly.

"This is just the beginning, I'll have to wait for a warmer day to apply the oil paint, too cold for it today. I'm thinking of making it summer in the painting; winter is just shades of gray, but in summer I can include the colors of the flowers your Mother plants and the ducks in the pond."

"Mother does do a wonderful job on this garden and it'll be good to see you capture it."

"What do you have there?" she asks as I take a drink from my cup.

"Hot chocolate from a vendor up the street. Would you like some?"

"Just having my hands on the cup would be wonderful, I think my fingers are frozen." She jokes but pushes her hands under her arms.

"Here, let me warm them up for you." I put down my cup and take my gloves off to undo one middle button on my jacket. I reach for her hands, but she draws back.

"Come nearer, I'm not going to hurt you."

She reconsiders with a smile and takes a step toward me. I remove her gloves and stuff both her hands into the warmth of my jacket.

"Oh my, it's quite lovely." She says as she looks into my eyes.

I'm taken a little aback by her nearness; her hands are warming nicely though and I no longer feel their coldness through my shirt. Moments seem to pass.

"I think they're back to normal now Patrick, may I have them back?" I hesitate a little before I realise what she's said.

"Yes...yes of course." She pulls them out and I pick up her gloves to replace them for her. When I finish, she returns the favor by reaching to button my jacket and tighten the muffler around my neck.

"Thank-you Patrick." she says softly.

"Anytime Bri, handwarming service at your disposal." I joke but the warmth of her hands remains on my chest.

"Well, I'd best be getting to the books." I say and walk toward the kitchen door, "Don't stay out here too long Bri, its getting windier."

"I won't." she calls back and when I turn before entering the house, she's watching me.

Amanda greets me in the library and looks up with mischief in her eyes.

"Doing a little hand-warming brother?" she asks as she looks back down to her paper.

"Okay, how did you....ah, the window." The draperies are still open until evening falls.

"Not that it's your concern sister, Briana's hands were very cold and it was hard for her to draw. I offered to warm them up, end of story." I coolly open a textbook pretending to forget the whole conversation.

"Patrick, Briana is a lovely young woman, you couldn't find any better friend. Just be considerate of her feelings and don't start something you don't intend to finish, okay?"

I look at my sister, "I won't Amanda. I respect Bri and would never do anything to cause her harm or concern."

◊◊

Continuing to the kitchen after my pause outside the library door, I am comforted as a mother by overhearing my son's speech to Amanda; seeing Patrick and Briana together through the upstairs window makes me realise my son is growing up and I'd best advise Daniel.

Mail is delivered later for Daniel, postmarked from New Zealand and I take it upstairs to slide under his door. Just as I turn to go, the door swings open and he appears.

"Mena, good morning."

"Oh Daniel, I thought you were out."

"I may have been mentally 'out' with all my work this morning, but I'm here." he smiles and asks, "Won't you come in?"

"Just for a moment, I have so much to do for the holidays, I don't know where to start." I enter but leave the door fully open, as decorum demands.

"How are your business plans going?" I ask and choose one of the chairs by the fireside.

"We have great groundwork laid, but weather conditions are holding up Angus' search for quarry sites. When it breaks, we'll start to move ahead again. How are you?"

"I'm good. We have a full house of visitors, but several are heading home or away for Christmas so only one or two will remain through the holidays. Please, read your letter, don't let me distract you." She urges.

"Only if you stay a little, I grow tired of talking to children and strangers all week and enjoy our conversations."

He opens the letter and his face lights up with what seems to be good news.

"My friend Ethan is a father again; a little girl, Bethany Anne. His wife Jane is doing fine."

He looks over at me. "Their son James was only twelve when Rose and I arrived, the next thing I know he's thirty and doing his internship in law.

"He and Ethan purchased our farm, mostly because James loves the land and continues to live there while he works as an attorney." He starts to read again.

"Thomas is doing great and has hired another blacksmith so he can run the mine fulltime."

Hesitating a little he says, "The rest is private, I'll just put this away for later. Now, what can I do to help for the holidays...I insist. You have your hands full with the Lodge and I want to help with the celebration."

"Well, it would be wonderful to have the help."

I really want to plan the meals with input from my 'fulltime family' which is the way I think of you and all 'our' children.

"Let's start tonight and have a fireside party after dinner. We can all talk about what we like to eat and where we'd like to visit, that sort of thing—what do you think?"

"Sounds like a great idea. This will be our first Christmas away from our friends and I want to make it special for the children in case homesickness sets in."

"You're very lucky Daniel. I have no relatives here in Aberdeen, all of them moved several years ago to Richmond, Virginia in America and I have no hope of ever seeing them again."

"What about your husband's family, no one you're close to?"

"Unfortunately, no. His parents passed and his brother moved to London with his wife."

"Then we'll just have to cover as your family this year Mena."

"You're already filling the position Daniel, as of a few months ago." I smile and place my hand on his as it rests on the chair arm. It feels so natural to sit with Daniel this way.

"Dad, you ready for dinner?" Angus comes around the corner of the doorway and stops short. "Please excuse me, I didn't know you had a guest, my apologies." he says, rather embarassed at seeing an obviously private moment between us.

"That's alright Angus, we were just making plans for Christmas and talking about getting everyone in our family involved." Daniel replies.

"I like it; assign some things to the 'younger' members, too, okay?" he remarks.

"Younger?!" Mena and I ask, pausing only a moment before we both toss a pillow at him. He ducks mine but Mena's grazes the top of his head.

"Whoa, that wasn't meant as an insult, I just meant we could do some work too." He laughs then withdraws to the kitchen for some lunch.

Our families meet later in the parlor after the other guests retire. I find the fire burning brightly and see Anna has placed coffee, hot chocolate and tea on the table with a tray of little cakes and pastries.

Mena sits on one settee and our youngsters on the other, looking at Briana's canvas. Something in Patrick's eyes as he talks to Briana and their full attention upon each other catches my attention.

I glance at Mena and she puts her finger to her smiling lips, signaling me not to comment on what she already knows. Well, well I think, my Briana is finally breaking out of her shell.

Chapter 13   Renewal

Angus enters the back door and takes the front stairs on the run, two at a time.

I hear his heavy footfalls then a cursory knock at my open door as he comes straight in, his face shining and flushed from the cold weather outside.

"What do you think of this?" he asks and unceremoniously puts a granite sample down in the middle of the papers on my desk.

I pick it up to put it in the sunshine spilling from the window. The sample is weighty and its color a light cocoa-brown with dark, almost black specks of mica through the grain. The mica is showy as it reflects the sunlight like a thousand small stars.

"It's different than any we've found so far and no visible layering which would cause it to split." I tell him. It appears to be a good stone for cutting and polishing I think and I look up at Angus who's fairly bursting to hear my comments.

"Son, I think you've found what we want; tell me about it."

He cheers a loud "Yahoo!" then continues his story.

"I rode between some farms out in the northwest shire this morning and stopped to speak with two residents, coming up with nothing. My last stop came just north of Inverurie, at a small farm of about twenty acres. I knocked at the door and a man older than you opened the door, Anthum McCrory."

"I feel better already, someone older than me."

"You know what I mean Dad. Anyway, I introduced myself and told him what we're looking for.

"He asked me in, then went to a shelf in the corner of the room. He brought this 'paper weight' to me and said he'd knocked it off a big rise of granite out in his field."

"You must have been amazed when he put it in your hand." I remark.

"I tried not to look too pleased, but I couldn't help it and asked him how much he thought was out there."

"What did he say?"

"He said, 'How much do you need, cause I doubt you could raise it all in your lifetime son." Angus pauses a moment at the memory of those bizarre words, then continues.

"Though the snow is on the ground, I asked him to show me the location. We walked out into the field toward a snow-covered barn, but which instead proved to be an upturned granite boulder.

"He told me he's never been able to successfully plow the field, the ground is shallow and the 'rock' runs all under it. Given its frozen condition, I couldn't take a shovel to it today, but I believe he's being truthful."

"This is good news son, you've done a great job. Now all we have to do is wait for the weather so we can get our surveyors out."

⊰⊱

The snow finally melted and it's been several weeks since Angus's discovery. The initial survey and analysis of the stone proved it was what we were looking for.

I put in our petition immediately for the new quarry and it was approved by the County Council. We finalized the twenty acre property purchase the next day and Mr. McCrory retired quite comfortably on his proceeds.

I've lined up a working partner in Harris Sebastian, a man recommended by John Hegge, who knew Harris professionally for several years out of a Glasgow quarry. Harris is charged to assist Angus with production practice and training and also see we're equipped with the latest steam-assisted equipment.

He'll set up a safe work program and cross-train the men; additionally he'll be a mentor for Angus in day to day operations.

Harris spearheaded the purchase of a steam-powered cutter for slab production and a powerful steam crane to move and load granite blocks and slabs for transport. As an extra bonus, he hired away the Glasgow quarry's steam specialist to maintenance all our equipment.

૰৺৹

During the last two months, a rail sidetrack to the quarry has been completed. With access to the Great Northern Railway, shipping to Aberdeen and its port, as well as connections with other railways in the U.K. are possible.

I'm handling the initial marketing and sales work for our unique granite and as soon as samples were ready, I distributed them to the various granite yards in Aberdeen for display. Orders began coming in almost immediately and production is increasing steadily every week.

I'll offer the granite to other yards in Scotland as soon as production is refined and we're running smoothly. The plan is to branch out to areas in the south; secure transportation routes via rail where available, with seaport to seaport, dray transport for isolated areas will be kept to a minimum.

My thoughts are interrupted as Mena appears at my door with a small package.

"Special delivery from London." She calls cheerily and drops it on my desk, supposing it to be something related to the Quarry.

"I'm going out to do some shopping, anything you need?" she asks.

"No, I can't think of a single thing, but thank-you for asking."

I turn my attention to the box after she leaves and sit up straighter to reread the postal address; 'Office of the Governor, Wellington, NZ'.

I cut the string and remove the heavy brown paper wrapping. I find a leather case and open it but set it on top of my desk and lean back in my chair. Inside, on dark blue velvet, is an Order of Merit medal. It is beautiful in design and similar to the Queen's Victoria Cross, one of the highest awards to British military staff for extraordinary valour.

I suspicion it comes through some action by Superintendant Anderson, but it doesn't make sense. I signed on as an unarmed volunteer citizen and was never formally called to service.

A folded envelope with the wax seal of the Governor of New Zealand lays in the wrapper and taking a deep breath, I pick it up to break the seal.

'From the Office of the Governor of New Zealand' it begins and is signed by Governor Sir George Bowen at Wellington. Many words down the page I find what I want to know.

'...as a civilian volunteer mediator for the Crown with native tribes in Otago during the period beginning 1850 and ending 1868, showed devotion to duty while performing under command of Superintendant George Anderson and did negotiate successfully with tribesmen in the Otago area, making concessions agreeable to both sides, resulting in a peaceful working relationship between the settlement and the Maori elders in that area.'

I refold it and put the letter in the top drawer of my desk then pick up the box to look at the medal more closely. I've never had a medal and don't think I deserve one now. Certainly I did what I felt was right to keep peace in our area, but I feel undeserving of such a grand award considering the men who actually fought and risked their lives in the North Island.

Not wishing to be ungrateful, I will accept it in acknowledgement of my life in New Zealand and in honor of my friend Teki Haku. I am very honored that Superintendent Anderson feels I am deserving.

I decide to store the medal away until the time is right to pass it on to Angus as a keepsake.

⁓

The Rosehill Quarry has become successful within its first year; much sooner than we had any right to expect. Setting up was intense work but it's been empowering to see my dream come true.

Too much time is being spent traveling and marketing, so I've relented, at Angus' insistence and hired a bonded accountant to handle the company books. True to my father's training though, I still review them regularly.

Angus, Kenna and Patrick graduate this lovely spring day of 1874. Mena, Briana and I sit eagerly with other parents and loved ones at the ceremony on the lawn.

They are finally called forward and approach solemnly. Angus receives his certificate and holds it high then waves to us after accepting his ribbon. Kenna receives a certificate of attendance and beams a lovely smile to us. Patrick waves at Mena then Briana.

Tomorrow, Angus leaves to live in the small house behind the company office and will run the Quarry as Vice President of Operations.

Kenna has already found an attorney in Aberdeen who's agreed to take her on for an entry-level position as a research assistant in his firm.

She knows she'll be thrown "left-overs" but is confident she will someday come into her own 'when society can understand and accept a woman's right to be anything she aspires to' as she puts it. It was difficult for her to put her legal career on hold and not to gain a degree in Law as her male counterparts did. But true to her strong character, she accepts it gracefully for the timebeing and is excited to begin her work.

Briana graduated with a degree in fine arts last year and true to herself, she couldn't forget her excitement over photography and finished a photo studio internship two months ago. She asked me earlier to invest in her business setup as a photographer upon graduation and because I love and believe in her, I agreed. It was a good decision; her classical painting enables her to compose backdrops for formal portraits no other in the area can offer. She exhibits her landscapes and still lifes in the shop and does quite well with them. She will go far, I am confident.

Patrick was offered an internship with a corporate law group in Aberdeen and happily accepted.

I travel once a week to Rosehill to meet with my partner Harris and Angus. We walk the quarry together and they bring me up to date on the week's production activities. Harris teaches Angus about steam and quarry work and in return, Angus teaches him about business and law. Their abilities have greatly contributed to the Quarry's success and make our meetings very interesting.

Surprisingly, I find my business interest sidetracked for the timebeing however, by a very different challenge; that of one Mrs. Philomena Gordon.

∾≫

At fifty-six years old, I've never thought to remarry but now face the fact I'm extremely fond of the auburn-haired Mena.

Anyone witnessing our present life would think we were already married by our routine. We spend evenings in the parlor at Hawthorne talking about our day and the children. We greet each other at the breakfast table with the other guests then go our separate ways and meet again in the evening for dinner.

Mena is different from Rose and I can't draw a comparison between the two; perhaps it's why I'm drawn to her.

She's a fiercely independent woman and used to being on her own in all aspects of life. She runs a successful Lodge, oversees employees, guests and every detail of the operation. Her finances are entirely under her control and from what I've observed during our stay, she's not a frivolous spender; except at Christmas, I chuckle to myself.

She takes excellent care of the Lodge and her family. Consequently, under her attention my young adults have grown to love her almost as much as I. Yes, I've admitted the fact to myself at last, but not to her.

So, on this summer evening when the roses in the garden are particularly fragrant, I decide to take her for a walk, on a mission unknown to her.

"Mena" I say as she holds my arm on our stroll down the stone path to the duck pond.

"Yes Daniel?"

"We've known each other for almost five years now."

"My goodness it hardly seems possible. You have your business now and we both have grown children graduated and out on their own."

I stop walking and she looks up at me.

"What is it Daniel?"

"I believe I love you Mena Gordon. In fact, I love you very much."

She smiles at me and searches my face.

"Truly Daniel? Then surely you know I love you too?"

"I hoped it would be your reply." I seat her on the bench overlooking the pond and bend to one knee.

"Philomena Gordon, will you do me the honor of marrying me, so we never waste another day of our lives in separate rooms?"

"I will, Daniel Smith." She reaches for my face and kisses me soundly before I try to say another word.

"But I have something for you," I say breathlessly after her kiss and stand to pull a small, round box from my pocket. I open it to show her a perfect blue diamond, surrounded by smaller white diamonds, all set in a band fashioned from New Zealand gold. Her breath escapes her for a moment as I put the ring on her finger.

"Daniel, it's beautiful. But you've spent much too much. A plain gold band would have been very suitable for people our age. Ah, but I do love it."

She puts her arms around my neck to hold me near and whispers "My dear Daniel, this is wonderful and almost more than my heart can bear." A tear slides down her cheek.

I whisper, "You're more than I could have hoped for my Mena" and kiss her warmly.

"The children will be here tomorrow for dinner, what do you think they'll say?" she asks.

"I think they'll say...'at last!'

"Oh Daniel!" she laughs and rests her head on my shoulder for a while.

Then we sit together in the twilight of the garden watching the waterbugs skate on the pond as the last rays of the sun turn the clouds and the water's surface golden.

Chapter 14 Angus

My desk is cleared and it's early evening but it doesn't matter, only a few steps to the cottage from here. I stare out the window at the Quarry's expanse, empty now that all crews are home with their families and probably sitting down to dinner.

The sun is setting behind the large excavation and the persistent dust stirred up by the evening breeze finally begins to settle.

I reflect on my growing business responsibilities; Harris hired two assistants for us just last month to help schedule and manage the minutia of eighty-five employees and though it's helped, we both know we'll need twice that very soon.

The union persists in their efforts to recruit our quarrymen, but so far none of our crews have done so. We pay top wages and true to our start-up plan, we keep safety uppermost. We've already designed and initiated safety masks to cut down on granite dust and the men are appreciative; one more reason they stand solidly against the Union at Rosehill.

My personal problems however, follow me out the back door every evening to my 'home'; tonight is no exception I think, as I lock up the office and walk the nineteen steps to the cottage our company provides.

The quiet darkness of the place gathers around me as soon as I close the door, as I knew it would. Increasingly I long for the noise and activity of the city, or even a town with its various characters would be refreshing. The Quarry is surrounded by hundreds of acres of farmland and I have no friends nearby; the closest town consists of a few homes and a church.

Hawthorne on the weekends is my salvation; its warmth and family make the weekends far too short and my trip back to the Quarry less than happy. As usual, my thoughts of Hawthorne bring Amanda to mind.

After graduation from university, she was unable to find a legal firm willing to hire her but when Kenna recommended her to her firm, one of the partners hired her on the spot.

It makes me smile to think how my sister has proven herself and made a difference in Amanda's life as well. It's been two years since university; she's now head of research at the firm and apparently both she and Amanda are bringing the senior partner into the modern age.

Amanda. Just her name makes my heart ache. I love her and have known it for some time. I've loved her from that first morning in Aberdeen when she entered the hallway, her red hair curling every which way after her bath and me feeling the fool in my night shirt.

One evening years later we sat enjoying the fireside in the parlor and laughed recalling that first encounter. We felt a bond then and knew something more existed between us, but the time wasn't right. We both had career aspirations which didn't include marriage, so we backed away.

Since then we're home on separate weekends and avoid the odd meeting that could bring us down a path to each other. She wants a career, I'm obligated to the Quarry business— end of story.

So I stand here tonight, alone and lonely.

"This is ridiculous" I declare and shake myself out of it as I slam a bowl out of the cupboard and fix some porridge for a quick supper before bed. I will find a solution starting tomorrow I promise myself.

The next day starts with a quick cup of coffee before I cut across the yard to the Quarry office. Dad's due in this morning for his weekly meeting and our regular walkabout of the operation.

Since he and Mena married, he leaves the marketing entirely to the salesman we hired. Dad celebrates his fifty-seventh birthday in a few weeks and we can well afford to pay for the extra position.

"Good morning...Daniel here yet?" Harris asks, as he enters from the Quarry.

"Not yet. I sent one of the men to the station to pick him up. How are you?"

"Good, no complaints. Things seem to be smooth downstairs on the floor, no one out sick." Harris replies.

"One of our foremen has a wife delivering," he adds, "expecting any minute, the midwife is with her and he asked to go home early. I sent him on his way with a shilling to pay the middy."

"Appreciate it Harris, need anyone to replace him?"

"No, not today, but we need someone tomorrow morning and I told him to be here bright and early. He's a good man, he won't disappoint."

"Good; the men appreciate your management Harris, several have sent their appreciation up the line for the way you handle things. Speaking of which, you've been more than patient in giving me on-the-job education; you know, the one not included with my degree?"

"Ach, you're welcome lad. You've held up your side of the bargain too, shall we just call it even?"

"Well said." I respond and we shake on it.

"Good morning gentlemen." Daniel says as he enters with a smile on his face.

"Hi Dad." I say and Harris goes to greet him.

"Good morning Dan."

"Are we ready to sit down to it?" Daniel asks. "I'd like to talk about any new equipment needs we should put in the next year's budget. And how about some coffee?"

We both laugh at his obvious energy this morning.

"Dad, how much coffee did you have at home?"

"Only two cups...really!" he adds, as he notices our looks of disbelief.

"Okay, if you say so. Let's sit down, but I'm getting you a cup of tea."

We settle in for a short meeting then take a break before walking down to the quarry to greet the men and watch the operation for a few hours.

When all is wound up for the day, Dad and I board a train at Inverurie and settle back for the trip into Aberdeen.

"So tell me Angus, how is life at the Quarry? I think of you frequently as I live in comfort with my Mena and wonder 'will this son of mine ever give me some wee grandchildren.' I meant it in humor, but I see something different cross his face.

"I'm not sure any woman would volunteer to live at the quarry father, therefore the prospects don't seem good."

"Angus, tell me what's bothering you."

He hesitates; we're alone in the train's compartment with no prying ears to overhear a private conversation and he looks at his watch.

"I find myself in a quandry Dad. There's someone whom I care a great deal about, but we're in circumstances which seemingly have no solution."

"And am I allowed to know who this wonderful person is?" I ask quietly but suspect I know.

"I don't think so, at least not yet. I need to explore any ideas you can suggest to break this deadlock because that's how I think of it.

"I'm living life without her and she has a successful career, but is alone as well. Nothing has been spoken openly between us, yet I feel certain her feelings are the same. She can't move out here from Aberdeen without leaving her job, nor would I want her to live in such spartan conditions.

"I can't live in Aberdeen and travel daily to the Quarry, the commute is long and it would cut my hours on the job, putting more on Harris. So give me a solution Dad." He finishes sullenly, making it clear he feels none exists.

"My, my...certainly a serious conundrum." I say thoughtfully. "Are you happy in your work at the Quarry, Angus?"

"I do enjoy my work, but I confess the isolation adds to my depression. I miss the city...I don't need the theatre every night, but I do miss taking a meal somewhere, walking out to the public library or museum once in a while.

"I miss living in a home with warmth and talking to other people about something besides granite." I finish rather abruptly and add, "I think I'm a little homesick."

"I think you are too, Angus. You're twenty-five after all and you've conducted yourself well in establishing a career; time to start rewarding yourself for your efforts."

"What do you mean Dad?"

"I mean, let's think how we can get you back to Aberdeen or within traveling range at least, so your heart's desire can be achieved. Life isn't all so complicated Angus, your heart is telling you to move and make something happen. You won't be able to deny it, at least not without becoming a bitter man. My advice; think it out and change it."

"But what about the quarry? I have to be there."

"Do you Angus? We've consistently hired the best of the best; our top foremen and the best crew money can buy. Yes, they need oversight but we have Harris and if he needs help without you on the premises, we can bring in someone to do it."

"I didn't think it would be possible."

"Here's what I think son; you've mistaken dedication for monkhood."

"Oh come on father, I'm just holding up my end of the business. You expect dedication and I hold myself to it." His face turns a little red as he talks.

"No, you misunderstand me son, you've done a fine job, but one thing I've learned about work and living life. A productive work life must be balanced with a successful private life. Are you happy? No? Then change it.

"Use the creativity I know you have and get yourself some happiness before it's too late. Shuffle the players, your work hours, do some hiring, within reason of course; do some life planning, the way you helped me plan the start-up."

Angus gets up to look out the window while I close my eyes and lean back in the seat. I remember the rocking of the train when we came to Aberdeen, how it lulled us to sleep. Hopefully, Angus will appreciate the trip this evening and allow himself to think outside the limits he's placed upon his life in the name of a career.

We arrive in Aberdeen station and decide to walk the distance to Hawthorne. The night is cool but comfortable and the walk is something we both need.

"I've thought about what you said and you're right Dad. I not only do my job, but I set myself impossible limitations in its name."

"Good, I'm glad to hear you admit it son. There is a balance everyone achieves to be happy; what would you like to do to achieve yours?"

We walk the way home together, sharing ideas which will inevitably change one life and perhaps even two.

 educ

The following Monday, I walk up Union Street to Amanda's office where the receptionist announces me. She comes to the outer office in a few minutes.

"Angus. What are you doing here?"

327

"I thought we might have lunch together, if you're able?"

"Why yes, nothing's happening on the schedule until this afternoon. What's the occasion?"

"I'm making some changes at the Quarry and I'd like to talk them over with you."

"I'm honored you would think of me. Just let me get my coat and we'll go."

We stop to purchase sandwiches from a sidewalk vendor then walk to a small park. It's busy with lunch-goers but we spot a bench where we can enjoy the sun's warmth while we eat.

"Did you know Patrick has taken a position in London?" she asks between bites.

"Really? That's exciting, when did this happen?"

"He saw an advertisement in the Times two weeks ago, sent them a response and they had him down for interview last week. He received a letter Friday they want him. He'll have to find a flat and all, but he's excited about it."

"Good for him, I know he's been ready to make a move down for some time." I finish up my sandwiche and turn to look at her.

"Amanda, Patrick's career change sort of compares with something I've come to realise recently...about us." She turns to look at me, her reaction one of surprise.

"Oh?"

"You may not realise it, or perhaps you do. Amanda, I've loved you for years and I've been stupid...for years."

She stops eating and puts the sandwiche down. "Angus..."

"Please, let me finish because this is taking all the courage I can muster just to get it out.

"I've loved you since we first met in the hallway at Hawthorne and have always thought as time passed, things like my career wouldn't continue to be a barrier. But now I know it's my mistake and it's not time which magically makes things possible, it's people."

"A very wise observation Angus, I've always thought that way myself."

"You have? The point is, I want time to mean something Amanda, not just pass by on the way to somewhere in the future. Father said last night 'everyone must balance life with work'. And in line with that, my first decision is to come to you and apologize for the way I've treated you since university. I've built a wall between us, but I do and will always care, more than you probably know."

"Oh Angus...this feels...it's sudden." She seems to struggle for the right words. "We've known each other for years and you're a true friend, a brother of sorts."

Not especially encouraging I think but continue to listen.

"Despite suspecting otherwise at times, I've been afraid to think of you in any other way. Let's walk, shall we?" She says.

"Yes, of course." I offer my hand to assist her up and keep the hand she gives me, tucking it under my elbow as we proceed around the park.

"The point is, I've watched you drive yourself so hard in your business, there didn't seem to be time left for anything else, including me. Do you ken what I'm saying Angus?"

"Yes, I do; in fact for the first time last evening on the train, when my father accused me of being a 'monk' in the guise of a business man."

"Angus," she shakes her head then can't help but smile and puts her hand on mine.

"I could never think of you that way."

"Encouraging Amanda, thank-heaven." I say it with humor, but really am grateful. "Starting today, I'm taking action to balance my life and work, starting with a move back to Aberdeen...for family, the town, but most of all to be closer to you.

"And in line with that, I'm visiting an agent today to see his listings for a place and I'd really like it if you looked at homes with me; your opinion would mean so much."

"I'd be honored to help you Angus. And about 'us'...give me some time to get reacquainted with the new you, alright?"

"Yes, of course. May I see more of you in my new balanced life?" I ask hopefully.

"I would like to, in fact, a new play is opening at the Music Hall tonight, why don't we attend. Now I really must get back to the office. Set up some house tours for tomorrow since we're both off and I'll see you at dinner tonight." She turns to leave, then faces me again.

"Here's something I have for you as a welcome home gift." She stands on her tiptoes and drops a kiss on my cheek then walks away down the sidewalk with a wave over her shoulder. I watch her as my hand lingers over the spot where her kiss landed.

This evening at Hawthorne it's black tie and dinner jacket for the theatre and tomorrow, I think with a smile, we'll look at some houses. I know I must be patient with her through the coming weeks; to expect otherwise would be disasterous. It's up to her now and I'm at her mercy, but it's a wonderful place to be.

I examine my tie to see it's straight and realise I still have a smile on my face. Apparently, the self-improvement plan is already working I note with satisfaction as I turn away from the mirrow to walk downstairs to dinner.

"Ah, here he is" Mena says as I enter the diningroom and see it's a small table tonight with only our family present.

"We have a celebration of sorts for Patrick tonight." she says proudly and looks at him. "My son has accepted a position in London."

I walk around the table to shake hands with him.

"Yes, so I'm told. Congratulations old man, Amanda told me at lunch today."

"I couldn't tell whether they liked me or detested me at the interview, Patrick exclaims with a laugh, "so it's a great surprise for me."

"When do you have to be down?" Daniel asks.

"I'll take the train Monday to see about a flat or something temporary and start the following week. I have no furniture so I'll probably look for something furnished."

"Tell me if you need anything, I know some people in the London furniture district; we've supplied granite table tops to them on occasion." Daniel volunteers.

"I will, thank-you."

Anna has outdone herself for dinner with two stuffed pheasants, garden vegetables and duchess potatoes. She bustles around the table serving everyone and adds her own congratulations to Patrick.

"My o' my sir, I remember you as a little boy, always so serious about everything. And now just look at you. All grown up and ready to move to the city on your own. Don't forget to come up once in a while and visit." She turns away to put something right on the sideboard.

"Now Anna, I could never forget this house or the people in it. Don't worry, I'll bring a healthy appetite home periodically for some of your cooking." He winks at Mena who knows Anna is family as much as any of us.

"I do have something else to add to this occasion." Patrick glances at Briana who smiles at him.

"Briana has consented to be my wife and Daniel has given his approval."

"I was very happy to give my fatherly approval, it didn't take much time to think about it." I smile at Bri's face so happy under Patrick's adoring gaze.

The room goes noisy with hugs, handshakes and good wishes. For just a moment my son Angus' eyes rest on the beautiful Amanda, dressed in her best gown for the theatre and sharing a hug with Briana. I can tell he longs to give such a declaration to the family himself, but theirs will come in time and he looks away before she notices his gaze.

"What about the store Bri, are you selling out?" I ask.

"No Dad, I'm definitely keeping it in the family. I'll hire a new manager and photographer to see to it before joining Pat in London. I'm going to start a new shop as soon as we're settled."

"Wonderful idea." I am so proud of her. Her photography is immensely popular in Aberdeen and I believe she'll be successful in London as well.

□□

The next day, Amanda and I tour three homes in the city, all granite of course, in the same area as Hawthorne and within walking distance of its back door.

One in particular appeals to us. Like Hawthorne, the house is updated with indoor plumbing and running water and very well taken care of. The three story sits on an acre of land facing a city park with a stable on the alley behind its small formal garden.

There's ample room with an office, a cozy library, a huge dining room, sitting room and efficient kitchen on the ground floor. Upstairs, are four bedrooms and a guest bathroom. In the master bedroom, we are surprised to see something new; an existing formal dressing room has been converted to include a large tub, sink and water closet, called a bath ensuite. The attic has built-in servants' rooms for four and a huge game room for long winters when guests need diversion.

"I think this will do very nicely, don't you?" I ask Amanda.

"It feels very welcoming Angus and the office is a large enough for you to bring work home."

"And for you to do the same Amanda." I say it before thinking. "...if you should call this home...at some time...in the future."

"It's okay Angus, I know what you mean and I appreciate your thinking of me. Now what about the stable, will you keep a horse? If not, it would make a great place for an office or studio, don't you think?" She glances slyly at me smiling innocently when I look at her.

"Why yes, for someone who wanted complete privacy, it would be perfect with a little renovation." I notice her eyes have gone soft and after a pause, I can't help but step closer to her. I look to see how she reacts but she takes a step closer as well.

"Amanda..." I start to say but she interrupts.

"Mr. Smith, I believe this girl is waiting to see what you are going to do next."

I do what I must and take the opportunity to kiss her, tenderly at first. The warmth between us is immediate and I kiss her again to sample her warmth further until I leave her lips gently.

When I open my eyes, her's are still closed and I smile, knowing we've connected for the first time. She opens them and we continue to gaze at each other.

"Angus," she whispers, "that was..."

"Yes..." I say, "it was."

But she returns to reality and takes a step back saying "We should be going."

"Yes, you're right." I reply and we walk outside to breath the cool, late afternoon air.

I sleep on the decision for the house and on Tuesday before leaving for the Quarry, I make a visit to the agent to put down a deposit.

I have a good feeling about it and wonderful feelings for Amanda.

Chapter 15 Decisions

I sit this morning rereading Ethan's letter which arrived yesterday.

I haven't mentioned its contents to Mena yet; she knows nothing about the mining in New Zealand and my children still don't discuss it.

Because we live so comfortably on the Quarry's income, I haven't thought it necessary to tell her about the gold or the invested residuals which are appreciating at an amazing rate. Even now it seems bizarre a poor laborer from Scotland can live the life we have.

I want to be open about our finances with her now though; not just because it's inevitable I won't live forever, but because I love her and want her to know I trust her in all aspects of our life together. The old days of keeping finances strictly a husband's business are passing away and should I leave this earth sooner than planned, I don't want her to feel I've concealed anything from her.

When my friends and I signed the mining company contract ten years ago, I had little confidence more gold would be found, but I was wrong. Ethan writes they've discovered a rich vein under the pastureland skirting the stream, one of the biggest strikes in the area.

Our contract is recently up for renewal and the mining company has offered to buy the Shell mine outright. Either we take their offer or renegotiate a new contract with updated terms; it's time for a decision.

Ethan and Thomas have already said they've been ready to retire for some time and wish to sell their shares. As for me, I'm unsure and would like to take a trip down to the Mining company's London office and speak with them in person. I'll take Kenna along, whom I trust implicitly to help negotiate a new contract, should that be my decision.

✄৩৽

The train to London pulls in on time; Kenna and I take a cab and arrive at the mining office by 11:45. Both of us have prepared to do some creative bargaining but to our surprise, an agreement is struck and a new contract drafted within a few hours.

I suspect the company appreciates my decision to continue with their services and have a feeling they've checked my net worth, seeing I could have my pick of mining companies, rather than choosing them.

The new contract retains one-third of the mine for my heirs and residuals from future gold pulled from the share. I added Angus to the contract to act in my absence. Ethan and Thomas will receive fair market value for a third of the mine, split 50/50.

After Kenna's review of the contract, I sign it and feel relieved the decision is made. Now it goes to New Zealand for Ethan and Thomas; the original name, the 'Shell Mine' is retained.

After returning from London, Kenna and I visit the bank to set up a new joint repository fund with Angus and me. My new Will directs the fund's residuals be split four ways between Angus, his sisters and of course Mena. I want my daughters to feel equal and secure in their own right as women and their husbands will have no claim to the monies.

Mena comes to the doorway, "Lunch my husband?"

"Sounds like a good idea, but first I have something to tell you."

"Hmm, mysterious. I love a good story." She sits down at my side.

"You're going to love this one." I say and proceed to relate we are millionaires, several times over.

❦❦

Ethan and Thomas signed the mine contract this morning in my presence; it signifies their release from the gold business for a final settlement of L250,000s each.

I'm happy for them and alarmed at the same time that Daniel's land will no longer be a farm, but a gold field dug up until every pasture is stripped and every bit of ore removed.

This evening I think of my promise to Daniel and the girls; the house is mine to protect and care for, but no longer possible...in its present location. I suddenly realise a solution; *I'll move it!*

∽❧∾

Barely able to sleep all night, I've decided to get Dad and Thomas involved in my plans, too.

"Ethan, James," Thomas greets us as we enter his shop, "alright, I know I'm in trouble when both of you visit at one time. Want to talk about gold today?" he asks with a smile.

"No, it's what the gold set in motion." I say and take a seat on a nearby bench. "We need to move Daniel's house and we need somewhere to move it to."

"You're joking." But he sees I am serious. "Okay James, what's this all about?"

"The mining company will destroy the pastureland and eventually the house. I want to buy new land and move the house so I can keep my personal promise to Uncle Dan."

"Alright, I understand, but you know moving the house won't be cheap, even if it's possible." Thomas says.

"I've saved my share of the farm's profit over the years and didn't really need it with my pay at the law office. I can afford a modest spread, maybe forty acres or less and I'll look in the farm's near vicinity so it'll just be a matter of moving it down a mile or two. Do I sound totally insane?"

"No more insane than I am for helping you." he replies.

"You will? You know the house will someday be of historic interest." I declare. Dad and Thomas both remain quiet.

"I mean it." I continue, "It's one of the first permanent structures in the settlement long before Daniel. How many can say they own such a thing? Practically everything here has been torn down or flooded out."

"After I move the house, I'm going to put a plaque by the door with the date it was built and names of the people who lived in it, the Rileys and the Smiths."

Dad comments, "Better add your own name there too, Son." He hesitates and rubs his chin before continuing, "I can see the forethought you've put into this, so I'll pitch in half of the moving expenses."

"I think you're right Ethan," Thomas speaks up, "I'll supply the other half, God help me, whatever amount it may be."

I laugh as Thomas wipes the sweat from his brow, "It's very generous of you both and a grand gesture, but I'm not holding either of you to it until we find out more."

"I do know this;" Thomas says, "no one in these parts can do that sort of moving. The house is granite and weighs several tons." He stops for a moment, then looks up at us.

"It might be cheaper to take it apart and rebuild it on the new site."

"Brilliant!" I exclaim. "Why didn't I think of it? It won't be easy, but it might be best. If we disassemble it, move the granite blocks by the load, we can hire a mason to oversee its reassembly on a new foundation."

"The only thing left," Dad adds, "would be to bring in a carpenter to put up the attic and roof. Something else, you'll have a chance to install indoor plumbing, too."

"You're right, I didn't think of that either. Once again, three heads are always better than one." I confirm enthusiastically.

In a few weeks, I find a forty-five acre farm for sale, just a mile north and on the opposite side of the road from Daniel's. The well, fencing, barns and outbuildings – are all in good shape. So it's a matter of removing the old rickety cob cottage and laying a new foundation.

A friend of my Dad's and a fellow Scotsman who's an experienced mason, has agreed to take on the task of deconstructing the house. He'll follow through with the reconstruction and I feel confident he'll do a good job or suffer my father's wrath.

❧

A year has passed and the house again stands firm on its new foundation, its attic, roof and new plumbing are complete.

I helped remove everything hand crafted and original to the house before its move and last week we brought everything back, right down to the two rockers infront of the fireplace.

This morning I push through my new front door to stand for a moment with suitcase in hand then remember to put it down. It's been over a year since I've truly felt at home, but I know it's where I am now.

During the reconstruction I stayed with Ethan and mum whom I love dearly, but I'm more than ready for my own space.

Ethan did a fine job overseeing the house project and its details when I couldn't get away from the office; everything in this room is as it was, except for the shiny new faucet beside the pump at the kitchen sink.

In the new bathroom behind the staircase, a copper sink, tub and new porcelain commode are installed; all are fed from a rainwater collection tank sitting on an eight foot high stand outside. *What will they think of next* I wonder then hear a knock on the front door and my family call out loudly.

"Hallo James...we're here."

"This is a surprise, what are you all doing? Hey, Thomas." They put several food baskets on the kitchen table.

"We're here to welcome you home and brought lunch." Mum says as she gives me a hug. My brother Michael pats me on the back and little Bethany puts her arms around my neck as I bend down to her level.

"Welcome home Jams', do you have any candy?" she asks in five year old innocence. Everyone bursts into laughter as I hug my little sister.

After lunch Dad brings out a letter he received last week.

"Here," he hands it to me, "it's from Daniel."

I begin to read, "He says he wishes he could be here to congratulate me on the house, but feels the trip would be too much and he couldn't handle the memories of Rose here." I find my eyes a little watery, so hand the letter off to Thomas.

Thomas reads next; "He's doing well, both Angus and Briana are married; Angus's wife Amanda is expecting in a few months and he doesn't want to miss that."

Jane reads next, "Kenna is working with a successful attorney in Aberdeen; imagine." she laughs, "Now that wouldn't have been allowed here." Then she hands the letter back to me.

"It means a lot just to receive this. I miss them all, but Daniel's like an uncle to me. I wish I could do something for him, maybe send him a gift or something. What do you think he'd like?" I ask them.

"He probably doesn't need a thing, always did live close to the bone." Dad says.

"You know," Thomas speaks up, "he might appreciate a fancy new desk since he owns a quarry; last I heard he's working at home on a writing desk in his study. You been in the furniture store lately? They have all sorts of desks made from some wood off the North island. It's beautiful stuff, you should go look at it."

"Maybe I'll stop by on Monday, thanks Thom."

❧

Before going to the office this morning, I decide to stop in at George Strickland's furniture shop.

"James, how are you? How's your Dad?" He greets me heartily.

"Just as lively as ever. Where's Joseph these days?"

"He's in India now. I worry about him, but what can a parent do."

"No use to worry, he's smart and trained well. He'll be okay George."

"Thanks James. What can I do for you today?"

"I'm looking for a desk as a gift, something unusual that can't be bought on the continent. Thom MacAndrew said something about some wood from the North Island?"

"Ah yes, Thomas visited last week and I know exactly what he looked at. The desks he saw are made of Kauri wood, top of the line stuff. Let me show you what we have over here."

I follow him to the side of the room and see three desks from small to very large against the wall. The largest catches my eye immediately; the luster of the wood is amazing and I've never seen anything like it.

"What kind of wood is this?"

"It's called Kauri; the natives dig it up. The logs are huge, in most cases from primal trees that fell into marsh mud and are preserved. It takes several teams of horses and strong men weeks to uncover. No telling how long the trees were in the mud but the wood is preserved perfectly.

"Various craftsmen turn it into furniture, including one from France. He's designed for Royalty, the King of England for one."

"You don't say. This one is beautiful." I say and run my fingers over its hand-rubbed surface and inset designs.

"It has a secret, would you like to see it?" George asks. "Stand here and I'll show you."

He puts his hand down on the right hand side of the desk. When he leans into it, a secret compartment opens out from under the desk's edge. It surprises me.

"How wonderful. Can I try?"

George closes the drawer and steps aside. I put my hand on the exact spot George points to and out pops the drawer again. I am absolutely fascinated by the device.

"I'd really like to have it, what's the price?"

"£240s and it's yours."

"I want to send it as a gift to Daniel in Scotland."

"Ah, Daniel Smith. Of course, a perfect gift. I understand he's a very successful business man in Aberdeen." He hesitates a moment, then says, "James, I want you to have this desk at cost; no arguments now, it would be my pleasure and will you pass along my good wishes to him, as well?

"I will George and thanks, I appreciate it. I'd like to write a brief letter and share the secret of the drawer with him. It would be a shame if he didn't take full use of the feature."

"I can arrange to have it shipped to Aberdeen if you have his address." George smiles.

"That would be perfect." I say with satisfaction.

Chapter 16 Closure

In late November a delivery rig from the docks pulls up to Hawthorne.

"Afternoon mam, I have a delivery for a Mr. Smith?"

"Yes, I'm Mrs. Smith. What in the world is it?" I'm amazed at the size of the wooden box lashed to the bed of his wagon.

"Says here it's a desk from New Zealand. Just sign here and let me know where you'd like it."

I ask him to wait a few minutes while I retrieve Daniel from the study.

"Daniel, there are deliverymen out front with a large shipping crate, a desk from New Zealand."

"What on earth," he questions,"Well, let's see to it."

❧❧

I follow Mena back to the front door and instruct the men to bring the box to the library where we watch them pry open the crate and remove the wood shavings used as packing. When at last the uncrating is finished and all waste removed in return for a handsome tip, we sit looking at the desk.

"It's quite grand isn't it Daniel," Mena remarks. "Look at the beautiful wood it's made from."

"Quite right, I've never owned anything to rival this."

I open the letter addressed to me from James.

"My, my. It's a gift from James in appreciation for, as he puts it, 'all the support through the lean times for my Mother and I and for being a wonderful Uncle.' I put down the letter and remove my glasses to quickly wipe my eyes, while Mena pats me on the back.

"He must think quite highly of you to send something like this to you."

"A good boy; manhood was thrust upon him at twelve years of age with the death of his father. He's an attorney now, with a weakness for farming." I continue to read that James has moved back into the farmhouse in its new location and George Strickland sends his regards as well.

"I think this calls for some sherry, what do you think old girl, a small glass?"

"That would be very nice." She smiles at me.

We drink a toast to James and George, Thomas, Ethan and all his family. Mena hasn't met them nor will she be likely to, but she holds them in high regard because they're my friends and it's enough for her.

It hasn't taken long since settling the desk in the library to stock it with my files and various supplies.

I've kept the secret of the drawer to myself; a man would like to have some mystery in life, I think in amusement.

Today, after some soul-searching, I approach the library shelf near the window to remove some heavy reference books and put them aside.

On the back of the deep shelf, I find the rough sack I placed there when we first arrived.

I pull out the jade talisman traded by Teki so many years ago with Rose. Its warmth lays in my palm for a few moments while I allow memories of her and our life together to fall like a gentle mist upon my soul.

Surprisingly, Tiki's friendship too, still so clear in my mind seems even stronger with the jade in hand though he surely must have gone on by now.

The old Colt pistol comes next from the sack; Ethan thought I would need this I recall, as I heft the weight of the old piece. I never needed it at all as it turns out, except the one time...and then I left it at home. *Life delivers its little jokes doesn't it*, I smile at the irony.

The secret drawer opens; I press the talisman to my lips then wrap it and the gun in a red linen scarf. The drawer holds both and I add a momento of my own before pushing it closed, knowing in my heart it will never be revisited.

"Daniel love, we're going to be late" Mena calls.

"Coming right along." I answer and stand up; my step is surprisingly light as I shut the library door behind me.

nd

Epilogue 1881

The midwife appears around the door.

"Come and meet your new son." She says cheerily.

I jump up from the tiresome bench outside our bedroom and go quickly to Amanda's side to take her hand. She's smiling as if labor and its pain were nothing more than a small inconvenience.

"I'm fine Angus, really - stop worrying."

"I can't help it my love." I bend to kiss her lips and search her face for the truth. The rosy glow on her cheeks and the sparkle in her eyes tells me she is indeed fine.

We both focus on the warm bundle in her arms. The darkest of hair is first admired and a little fist finds its way out of the bunting to seemingly shake at the world. We laugh at the gesture as our hearts are wholly drawn to our creation.

"What shall we name him?" I ask and watch him fall back asleep.

"I would love to include my father's middle name, 'Regis.' Amanda says. "He was a wonderful father and we would be so blessed if any part of him happened to be in our child."

"Very well, I think it's an excellent idea."

"Then, Regis Angus?" she asks, looking into my eyes.

"Good idea. It'll reduce the chance of confusion whenever calling 'Angus' in the household." I joke and Amanda shares my humor with a smile then adds, "Regis Angus has quite a royal sound to it, doesn't it?"

"He is royalty, he's our son." I reply and gladly linger by her side to watch him sleep.

Coming Soon

COPPERSWIFT

'What if more exists in this house than we've discovered I ask myself and stop reading the records Donnie sent from Aberdeen yesterday.

My eyes stray to the contents of the old desk compartment on the corner of the table, except the gold nugget which Stephen has locked up in the family safe.

I feel in the pit of my stomach there's more to this, but what?'

≈Sarah as she works in the library at Highbridge.

Return to Highbridge Manor to check in on Sarah, Thomas and the rest of the family you loved in Windows. Will they marry as planned? Is the Mill a success? Will Sarah find the answers she needs to complete Stephen's history?

If you've enjoyed Daniel Smith, please leave a brief review at one or more of these sites or simply 'Like' the book.

LindaJPiferauthor.com

Goodreads.com

Amazon.com

www.ingramcontent.com/pod-product-compliance
Lightning Source LLC
Chambersburg PA
CBHW051528250626
47156CB00001B/277